THE
KITE
RIDER

'McCau... ...which
historic... ...s;
China's rigid family laws; the harshness of a child's life in the 13th
century—runs alongside a fiction so imaginative that it is like a dazzling
chimera.'

Nicola McAllister, Saturday Telegraph

'Geraldine McCaughrean is one of the finest writers of today. Her
imagination soars. The reader is almost physically transported to the
teeming seaport of Dagu, and the towns on the long length of the Hai
River to vividly experience life among the Mongols, and at the court of
...rd Khan. The book is a delight.'

Iona Opie, The School Librarian

...ook, set in 13th century China, is a marvellous, soaring story that
...ou a glimpse into another world . . . A wonderful, dense novel,
... with the truth that part of loving your parents is knowing how to
...them.'

Lyn Gardner, Guardian

...work of astonishing energy and inventiveness . . . packed with
...and intrigue, this is an exhilarating new novel from an author
...ever disappoints.'

The Times Educational Supplement

...f daring and danger, and suffused with local sound and colour,
...a children's novel on an epic scale.'

Robert Dunbar, Irish Times (Dublin)

...is a novel about breathtaking sacrifices, about love, courage and
...dship set against lust, violence and avarice. It snatches you up from
...rst chapter, and like Haoyou riding his kite, carries you up into a
...that is shocking, beautiful and compulsive.'

Sunday Times

...first class reading—absorbing, enjoyable and unforgettable'

Time Out Kids Out

... this novel has an atmosphere so compelling that it is impossible to
...arate exotic fact from inspired invention . . . continually exciting, and
...lamentally compassionate'

The Weekend Review, Independent

'The detail is phenomenal but unobtrusive, the narrative warm,
sometimes humorous, and consistently compelling.'

Guardian

'The book has two main themes. One is the family, the spiritual power of its dead and the often undeserved, misused authority of its living seniors, and the onus of duty and obedience on the young . . . The other theme is the fear and ecstasy of flight . . . The two subjects blend in an original and exciting story.'

Books for Keeps

'Enticed into the story from the start, the reader is transported to a magical time rich in history and folklore. He is treated to all the poetic mystery and charm of an Eastern fairytale.'

W4Kids

'McCaughrean brings alive a society where human life is cheap, and where disobedience to a parent is punishable by death, yet where kindness and creativity survive. A masterpiece of storytelling for 10 years up.'

The Times

GERALDINE McCAUGHREAN

THE KITE RIDER

OXFORD
UNIVERSITY PRESS

For John and Ailsa

OXFORD
UNIVERSITY PRESS

Great Clarendon Street, Oxford OX2 6DP

Oxford University Press is a department of the University of Oxford.
It furthers the University's objective of excellence in research, scholarship,
and education by publishing worldwide in

Oxford   New York

Auckland   Cape Town   Dar es Salaam   Hong Kong   Karachi
Kuala Lumpur   Madrid   Melbourne   Mexico City   Nairobi
New Delhi   Shanghai   Taipei   Toronto

With offices in

Argentina   Austria   Brazil   Chile   Czech Republic   France   Greece
Guatemala   Hungary   Italy   Japan   Poland   Portugal   Singapore
South Korea   Switzerland   Thailand   Turkey   Ukraine   Vietnam

and associated companies in Berlin   Ibadan

Oxford is a registered trade mark of Oxford University Press
in the UK and in certain other countries

British Library Cataloguing in Publication Data available

ISBN: 978-0-19-275528-5

9 10 8

Printed and bound in Great Britain

Paper used in the production of this book is a natural,
recyclable product made from wood grown in sustainable forests.
The manufacturing process conforms to the environmental
regulations of the country of origin.

Cast of Characters

The Gou Family
Great-Uncle Bo, head of the family
Great Aunt Mo, his wife
Pei, a sailor, nephew of Bo Dong
Qing'an, Pei's wife
Haoyou, Pei's son, aged 12
Wawa, his little sister
Mipeng, a distant relation, a young widow and a medium

Di Chou, first mate aboard Pei's ship

Miao Jié, or 'The Great Miao', circus master of the Jade Circus
Bukhur, a Mongol bird-catcher
Khutulun, his daughter

Kublai Khan, Mongol conqueror of thirteenth-century Cathay (China)

The Song dynasty, Chinese rulers of Cathay before Kublai Khan's invasion

1

Testing the Winds

Gou Haoyou knew that his father's spirit lived among the clouds. For he had seen him go up there with a soul, and come down again without one.

It happened down at the harbour, the day the *Chabi* put to sea. When she set sail, Haoyou's father, Gou Pei, would be among her crew and gone for months on end. So Haoyou went with him, down to the docks, to make the most of him on this, their last day together. 'When I get home this time,' said Pei, 'we must see about *you* becoming an apprenticed seaman.'

Haoyou's heart quickened with fear and pride at the thought of stepping out of childhood and into his father's saltwater world.

For the first time ever, Pei took him aboard—showed him where the anchor was lodged, where the sailors slept, how the ship was steered, where the cargo would be stowed. And the biggest excitement of all was still to come: soon, the *Chabi*'s captain would be 'testing the wind', checking the omens for a prosperous voyage.

Further along the harbour wall, a great commotion started up, as a ship, newly arrived from the South, disembarked its passengers: a travelling circus. For the first time in his life, Haoyou saw elephants, ponderously picking their way across the gangplank, while tumblers somersaulted off the ship's rail and on to the dockside.

1

There were acrobats in jade-green, close-fitting costumes, twirling banners of green and red, and jugglers and stilt-walkers, and a man laden from head to foot with noisy bird cages. There were horses, too, ridden ashore across the sagging gangplank as recklessly as if it were a pack bridge, by Tartar horsemen in sky-blue shirts.

'Ragamuffin beggars,' grunted Haoyou's father—which made Haoyou laugh, since the gorgeous circus people, finding his father's tattered, rice-straw jacket, would probably have fed it to one of their elephants. The Gou family was not exactly the cream of elegant Dagu society. Still, he sensed that he should not ask to see the circus perform: circus people were obviously not *respectable*—especially when they included Tartars.

The ship on which his father Pei was about to set sail had a Tartar name now. Last season she had had a perfectly good Chinese name, but in an effort to curry favour with the conquering barbarians, the captain had renamed her after the Khan's favourite wife: *Chabi*. Pei muttered gloomily about it. Her hull had been re-timbered, a new layer of wood hammered on over the old, so that she was beamier than the year before. 'It looks as if the Khan's wife has been eating too many cakes,' said Pei. He laughed and put a loving arm round Haoyou's shoulders.

'Impertinent dog,' said a voice close behind them, and the *Chabi*'s First Mate took hold of Pei by his jacket and pushed him over the edge of an open hatchway.

It was no great way to fall, but Pei landed awkwardly, his leg twisted under him, and lay gasping on top of the sacks of rice which were the ship's provisions. Haoyou went to the hatchway and lowered one leg over its edge, going to the help of his father. But the First Mate took hold of him by the collar, wrestled him along to the gangplank, and threw him off the ship.

Haoyou wondered whether to run home and tell his

2

mother, or stay and see what happened. His father injured on the eve of a voyage? It was not good, not lucky. Lucky for Haoyou (who hated his father going away for months on a voyage), but not for the family dependent on his sailor's wages.

Haoyou decided his mother should know, and turned to run. But he found his way barred by the corpulent bellies of the merchants mustering on the dockside. Word had gone out that the *Chabi* was testing the wind this morning, and it seemed as if every merchant in Dagu had hurried down to judge the omens for themselves. The prosperity of the whole voyage depended on how the 'wind-tester' behaved. Only if it flew well would they entrust their cargoes to the *Chabi*. If it flew badly, they would use some rival ship.

It was for this magnificent sight that Gou Pei had brought his son to the harbour; Haoyou had asked a hundred times to see it.

'I'm not sure,' his mother had said. 'What about the poor soul on the hurdle?'

But Pei had only shrugged and said that worse things happened at sea.

Haoyou looked back at the ship. He did not want to miss the testing of the wind. Perhaps his father had only twisted his ankle, and would be fit to sail after all. The boy stood on tiptoe to estimate the depth of the crowd; his chances of pushing his way through them. None, he decided, and stayed where he was.

A strong, gusty breeze was blowing. Members of the crowd held up wetted fingers and nodded sagely. All the signs were auspicious. A bright, cheerful sunlight brightened all the colours in their silken clothes, bleached the rust-red sails of the *Chabi*.

A foreigner stood among the crowd—neither Chinese nor Mongol, but a tan-coloured man with eyes shaped like a horse or a dog. The Chinese man alongside him was explaining the process of testing the wind.

'A hurdle is hooked to the end of a rope and set flying in the breeze . . . '

'Like a flag?' asked the foreigner.

'Not a flag exactly . . . More like a kite. Pardon my foolishness: I don't believe you have the word in your language: "kite". As the men tug on the rope's end, the hurdle rises up higher and higher on the wind. If it rises up straight, the voyage will prosper. If it flies out so . . . '—the guide's hand, in darting out at an angle, dislodged Haoyou's cap—' . . . there may be problems.'

'Problems?'

'Storm, perhaps. Becalming. Pirates. Shipwreck.'

The merchants standing shoulder-to-shoulder with the guide eased themselves away from him as he spoke the words of calamity—as if the words themselves might carry bad luck.

Suddenly the tall foreigner with the horse eyes gave a cry. 'You did not tell me about the *man!*' Haoyou smiled secretly at the foreigner's surprise.

The hurdle—a big square hatch-cover woven out of palm leaves—was being carried along the deck by seven or eight sailors. The rope was already attached to it by a harness of four cords shackled to each of the four corners. Also bound to this giant kite was a man.

A cloth had been wrapped round his head, but now, as he twisted this way and that, struggling to break free, the cloth slipped down and Haoyou caught a clear glimpse of his face.

'*Father!*'

The crew must have been pouring rice wine into Pei because the muscles of his face looked slack, and there were stains on his chest. But his pinioned hands opened

4

and closed, and the tendons of his bare feet were as rigid as birds' talons.

'Do they employ criminals for this?' the foreigner enquired.

'No, no. Just one of the crew—either very drunk or very stupid.'

The horse-eyed foreigner nodded and began sketching on a piece of paper, drawing a diagram of the kite harness.

'*Let him go! Untie him! You leave him alone!*' shouted Haoyou, and struggled to get back on board. But a stevedore carrying a sack of salt had set it down at the top of the gangplank and sat down to watch the testing of the winds. The gangplank was blocked.

'*Father! Don't let them! Let him go, you demons!*' But the noise of the crowd swallowed Haoyou's voice like the sea swallowing a whisper. He could not make himself heard.

Should he run to fetch his mother? By the time he reached her, the kite would be aloft. Should he avert his eyes from the humiliation of his honoured father? Haoyou could no more have looked away than a dead man can close his own eyes. He saw the hatch-cover carried up to the bow and angled so as to catch the full force of the wind. He saw its woven fabric flex and bow, and his father's hair spread itself around his head as if glued fast to the hurdle.

With a noisy rattle, the wind-tester shed gravity and rose into the air on a gust of wind, tautening the rope. The crew paid out more, then, as the hurdle tilted, jerked on the rope so hard that Pei's jaw snapped shut. The hurdle caught the wind again and rose straight up—thirty metres, forty. Haoyou could see that his father was shouting, but the wind snatched the words away and left only the black circle of Pei's mouth.

Then the gusty breeze failed. Momentarily, the kite

veered and slumped, dropped down towards the crowded quay. People gasped and ducked, arms over their heads.

Haoyou did not duck. His face, still upturned, saw his father plunge towards him face-first, eyeballs straining their lids, arms spread wide, head and shoulders buckled outwards from the hurdle. Those eyes focused on Haoyou, recognized him, and the boy saw his own name form on the mouth which hung over him. Like a rabbit overshadowed by a hawk, Haoyou was powerless to move. *'Father!'* Haoyou called back. Then the crew of the *Chabi* yanked on the rope once more—such a jerk that Pei bit through the tongue still pronouncing Haoyou's name. The giant kite lurched into a gust of wind and soared upwards, drawing a gasp of relief from the crowd. Up and up it climbed, straight over their ship, leaning to neither right nor left but climbing higher and higher, until Pei's shape was no more than a blur beyond range of Haoyou's eyes. He dragged his knuckles through his lashes to be rid of the tears, but still could not see. The wind-tester had climbed to such a height: when it steadied itself in the smooth continuous winds of the upper sky, it was no longer a man on a hatch-cover, lashed to a ship's cable, but a money spider on the end of a silken thread.

The crowd murmured its approval. The voyage of the *Chabi* would be prosperous. A cargo entrusted to this fortunate ship would reach its destination in safety and bring a good profit.

Strands of straw drizzled out of the sky, falling on to the faces of the crowd. Idly the merchants pulled strands out of their hair or brushed their shoulders. It conveyed nothing to them. But Haoyou let the fragments of his father's rice-straw jacket rest on his face and shoulders like a blessing. His father was among the clouds, and Haoyou did not feel entitled to so much as breathe until the flight was over.

What was Pei seeing up there, in the province of the birds? Could he see Haoyou's little board-built house and his mother hanging out the washing or shelling peas for the cooking pot? Could he see the white furrows ploughed by ships, and the shoulderblades of whales hummocking the ocean? As far as the Imperial City? The island of Japan? Could he see into the Past or into the Future?

The crowd began to mix and moil, merchants shouting to their secretaries, factors shouting to the warehousemen, money-lenders offering terms of credit. The first sacks of salt were being carried over the springy gangplank by agile barefooted stevedores. Haoyou was jostled and pushed out of the way. Still his face was upturned, his thumbs trapped inside his fists, his eyes on the tiny, distant kite, as the crew hauled it in.

They worked with no great urgency. The urgency was over: the captain had secured a prosperous voyage. So they wound in the kite slowly, like old women skeining wool. Little by little, the hatch-cover became visible for what it was, its passenger taking on detail: the colour of his trousers, the tilt of his head. The lower it got, the more the wind tossed it about, to left and right. At last the breezes failed to hold it and it slammed down into the sea, narrowly missing the harbour wall. It floated passenger-uppermost, and Pei was jarred and jolted as the crew scuffed it across the surface of the water. As it scraped and banged against the ship's hull and was pulled aboard, Haoyou dashed between two stevedores and crossed the bendy gangplank in nimble strides. 'Father! *Father!*'

Pei had returned to earth with the hatch-cover. His eyes were still open, his lips still drawn back from his teeth in shouting. But his spirit had remained among the birds. Somewhere during the flight, his heart, over-crammed with fear, had burst like a sack of grain and his spirit had been spilled into the path of the prevailing easterly winds.

Only tatters of his rice-straw jacket encircled his armpits, and the skin of his bare stomach showed, tinged with the blue of cold and death. To Haoyou, though, it seemed as if his father's body had taken on the colour of the sky.

The crew, who had known and liked Pei, began to mutter syllables of sorrow and regret, slapping out at Haoyou with sympathetic hands. One even ran to snatch feathers from a chicken running loose about the deck, and held the feathers to Pei's lips, hoping for signs of life. The feathers fluttered in the wind, but not with the passage of breath.

'He was a good man, your father.'

'Di Chou should never have . . . '

'Fate is hard, boy.'

But the *Chabi*'s captain, not wanting a death to detract from the favourable omens of the kite's flight, sent the First Mate to break up the little knot of mourners.

'Get rid of him and sign a new man in his place,' said First Mate Di Chou. 'And the rest of you . . . get back to work.'

Haoyou flung himself at the man—a brute as thickset and sturdy as a bollard, with a round, neck-less, bollard head. *'You sent him up there! You killed him!'* Haoyou shouted, pummelling the flat, unyielding stomach, bruising his fists on Di Chou's leather belt.

Di Chou took hold of Haoyou by the ear, and the shining flesh of his cheeks twitched with menace, as he smiled down at the boy. 'Your pretty *mother* needs telling, boy. She's a widow now. Tell you what, boy . . . I'll come myself and tell her. These things shouldn't come from a stranger. A woman needs a friendly face at a time like this.'

2

Troubled Spirits

Haoyou's mother, Qing'an, was a woman of uncommon beauty. Pei's relations had nudged one another at the wedding and stared, astonished that a mere deckhand had achieved such a bride. His ageing and ugly aunts and great-aunts shook their heads, implying that no good would come of it, comforting themselves that the bride's family was destitute and of no repute. But his cousins and uncles had simply looked, mouths ajar, savouring this new adornment to the family, as they would a rare and beautiful vase on the family shrine.

Now they were gathering again, for her husband's funeral, startled by the manner of Pei's death but unstartled by death itself. It was a common enough event among the poor of Dagu's waterfront.

'A sailing man is lucky to have had such a dry death,' Great-Uncle Bo intoned in his croaking, bullfrog voice.

His thin wife, Mo, ducked her thin head in agreement. 'It is harder for a widow when her man is lost at sea and she has no body to mourn over.'

Did they think this was easy, then, for Qing'an? This jostling invasion of distant relations eating the last food out of her storage jars? Most had not visited Pei and Qing'an since the naming of their first child. They marvelled now that Haoyou had grown to such an age without acquiring any more brothers: only one small, worthless sister.

'The woman has obviously been trying to keep her

figure,' Haoyou heard a florid woman confide in a hoarse, envious whisper. So. They still envied Qing'an, these coarse-featured gossips, even now that she had lost her helpmate and breadwinner: the love of her life.

Haoyou did his best to be a good and useful son. He had made all the paper images for the funeral: little paper cut-outs of jacket, trousers, rice-bowl and chopsticks, rice-wine bottle, hand barrow, sandals, and fish. He had even cut out a dog—though the family had no dog—because he thought his father might like one in the next life. He had crafted a double-layered, full-length coat, and a fishing rod threaded with a single strand of silk and baited with a shred of feathers; a little model coracle, too, out of gum-soaked silk, with a rudder of split bamboo. Now, in the afterlife, his father could spend his time doing the kinds of things he had never had time to do during his lifetime.

'They are very well made,' said a hollow-eyed young woman in an ankle length tunic. She was holding Haoyou's little sister in her arms. Haoyou could not place which branch of the family she belonged to.

'They are nothing,' said Haoyou, which was the proper and polite response to a compliment.

'Oh! Did you make them? I thought they came from a shop.' The girl ducked her head and spoke to the child in her arms. 'You have a clever brother, little Wawa. Does he make things for you?'

Wawa smiled rapturously and gave a wriggle, wanting to be put down. Off she went, out of doors, her wrap-round apron showing her bare plump legs from behind. Cheekily she pushed between the legs of the assembled guests, unaware of the reason they were there, cluttering her yard, upsetting the chickens, eating party food.

It was in watching her go that Haoyou caught sight of the familiar straw sandals and sailcloth breeches of Di Chou.

10

Someone set off a crackling, rip-rap firework alongside his father's shrine, but Haoyou thought the explosion was inside his head.

'What's the matter?' asked the hollow-eyed girl.

Haoyou should have said nothing. No one speaks to a stranger at a funeral: they just chatter idly. But he was caught off guard. 'Why is he still here? The *Chabi* sailed yesterday. Why isn't he gone?'

'Who?'

With a nod of his head, Haoyou pointed out the First Mate, who was in deep conversation with the head of the family, Great-Uncle Bo. There was no mistaking those buck teeth, the long necklace of mummified animal parts, the tattooed pig on his hand. 'He killed my father,' said Haoyou.

The rip-rap firework burned out. A single rocket, propped up in an oil bottle, shifted in a gust of wind. The bottle overturned and the rocket went off, like a hornet, ripping between the startled heads of the funeral guests and hitting the chicken coop with a noise like Mongol artillery. One chicken was killed outright. The rocket passed within a hand's breadth of little Wawa, who had just come back with an example of her brother's handicraft to show the hollow-eyed lady.

The kind lady had asked if her brother made toys for her; so she had brought the kite he made for her second birthday—the one with a carving of a little man hanging on beneath it. Now Wawa stood stock still, terrified by the stray rocket, the kite clutched to her chest, her little fingers inadvertently pushing through the paper.

The crowd drew back from her, with a gasp of superstitious dread. A kite with a man aboard it? At the funeral of a man who died aboard a wind-tester?

Then the hollow-eyed lady darted forward and swept Wawa up into her arms, tickling her, blowing in her ear, admiring the pretty toy. 'Did your brother make this? What a clever brother! Lovely colour . . . just like a butterfly. Let's just take it outside . . . '

Haoyou was still staring at the tattooed First Mate, wording and rewording what he could say to denounce out loud this wicked, pitiless, bullying beast of a man. How dare Di Chou come and eat the bake-meats at the funeral of the man he sent to his death? Haoyou's mouth was too dry to choke down the rice cake he was holding. It lay in his hand, forgotten. The sweat in his palm was making it sticky.

A gull on a neighbouring roof saw its opportunity and glided down through the perfumed haze of the shrine, the cordite fumes of the fireworks, the smoke from neighbourhood rubbish burning. Big as a cat and with sulphurous yellow eyes, it struck Haoyou in the face with its great moulting grey wings as it snatched the cake out of his hand and flew back to perch on the roof.

And all of a sudden the guests were leaving. Here was one unlucky omen too many. They did not exactly make a dash for the street, but formed themselves into an impatient queue, lining up to mouth their regrets at Haoyou's mother:

'Our fates are written . . . '

'No one escapes his destiny . . . '

'When our ancestors summon, we have to go . . . '

As they spoke their platitudes, they thrust their empty rice-wine cups and plates of bake-meats into the widow's hands, such was their hurry to be gone. Even the hollow-eyed girl seemed to have fled the blighted party.

Qing'an emptied her hands of crockery, sat down beside the chicken coop and wept, rocking her head against the splintered wood. Haoyou did not know whether it was for his father, for the dead chicken, or for want of any loving relations to comfort her. He had never seen her weep openly before, in front of him, and he had no idea what to do, other than avert his eyes and sidle awkwardly back into the house. In the doorway he collided with the hollow-eyed girl.

'I put your little sister down to sleep,' she explained, holding up a hand alongside her face, so as not to shame her hostess by seeing her cry. 'I weep for your sorrows,' she said, and was gone, skittering out into the lane on her little wooden pattens. With some part of his brain, Haoyou was aware that only she, out of all the women at the funeral, had been wearing pattens rather than straw slippers. She alone walked raised up above the dirt and litter of the dirty, dockside lanes.

When Haoyou woke, he tried to move so fast that his dream could not cling to him. He determined to shake it off by the sheer speed with which he scuttled out of bed, fetched in the water, brought it to the boil. He concentrated entirely on pouring the hot water into the two cups, without spilling a drop, sprinkling the tea leaves in exactly equal numbers on to the steaming liquid. He spaced two of the cups in the precise centre of the tray, and carried it so carefully that not a single drop spilled. Then he circled the partition to where his parents' bed lay beneath a grey-morning window.

'Good morning, honoured mother and father,' he said, as he had said a thousand times.

Then the tray fell from his hands with a crash, and he stood staring at the shards of pottery, the spreading puddle of tea. He had been trying so hard to bury his dream under everyday routine that everyday routine had undone him. This was the day after his father's funeral, and he had forgotten his father was dead. 'I'm sorry! I'm sorry! I didn't mean to say it! I forgot! No! I mean, I didn't forget. Of course I didn't forget, but . . .'

His mother sat up, still wearing the clothes of the previous day. It was plain she had not slept. She held out her arms and Haoyou ran to her, like a boat running for harbour in a storm.

'I dreamt there was this cormorant!' he sobbed, chafing his cheeks against the seam of her jacket, the embroidered birds and flowers. 'A big black cormorant! I dreamt it came swooping down on me, and I was going to be swallowed, and I couldn't move! I couldn't move! *And it was him! It had his face, Mama! It was horrible!'* Haoyou tugged at the metal collar he wore round his throat, his own fingers making it bite into his windpipe and increase his panic. 'I was going to be swallowed— like a fish!'

His mother's hand stroked the back of his head, over and over, and she shushed him as she would a fractious baby. 'I'll sew you a tiger on your jacket. A new tiger,' she said, 'to frighten the bad dreams away.'

Already his jacket was a menagerie of animals, the colours of the threads faded to a greyness, along with the coat. As he outgrew one jacket, its embroideries were cut out and incorporated into the next one, its oldest animals preserved since the days of his babyhood. He had given them all names. His hand closed automatically now over Wu the Dog. But Haoyou did not think even Wu would be able to make things right this time.

' . . . and after that, I shall send for the medium,' his mother was saying.

'Pardon?'

'It's lucky we have one in the family. She may only charge a little.'

'We have a medium in the family? Who? Why do we need a medium, Mama?' The embroidery dog beneath his palm seemed to bristle with fright. The hand on his neck trembled as it stroked his hair.

'Well, Haoyou, it's plain your father's spirit is angry. All that trouble at the funeral. Now this dream of yours: your father coming to you, like a black bird . . . And the broken cups. Your father's spirit is trying to tell us something. We must find out what he wants.' She had lowered her voice to a whisper, as if her husband might even now be eavesdropping outside his own bedroom: he from whom she had never kept a secret while he was living.

'No, you don't understand . . . ' Haoyou began.

'Hush,' said his mother soothingly. 'Mipeng will know. The medium will know what we have to do. You mustn't worry.'

'You don't understand!'

But his mother was preoccupied, wondering what she could sell to pay for the medium's advice.

And now that Haoyou thought back, of course his mother was right. Everything pointed towards it: a restless spirit, an unhappy spirit, a malevolent spirit demanding something from those left behind in the living world. The toppling firework, Wawa fetching in the unwelcome kite, the thieving seagull, the dead chicken . . . It hardly seemed worth correcting her about his dream.

But the face on the nightmare cormorant—fixing him with its beady eye, gaping after him with its serrated bill—had not been his father's.

It had been First Mate Di Chou, his father's killer.

3

A Proposal

First Mate Di Chou had let the *Chabi* sail out of port without him, because there was quite another vessel he wanted to board.

Ever since the first time he had seen Qing'an standing tiptoe on the quayside to catch sight of her home-coming husband, Di Chou had made up his mind to have her.

Pei had been loath to talk about his good fortune, for fear of tempting the gods. But there are ways of reading a man's true thoughts by the efforts he makes to hide them. 'My ugly wife? Idle the whole day,' Pei had always said. 'She makes the house a midden with her laziness. Cooks like Genghis Khan—old goat meat underdone. The children are no better.' But if the gods were fooled, Di Chou was not. Qing'an was the kind of woman who made her husband run from the ship past four inns and a gaming house, just to wrap her in his arms.

Somewhere, at the end of some festering waterway, in a landscape of paddy fields, Di Chou also had a wife. But he happily praised her aloud, day and night, in the hope that the jealous gods would snatch her and her sickly brats up to heaven. Fortunately Di Chou had out-sailed his past—left it far enough behind him that none of his shipmates even knew he was married. He told each quartermaster, as he signed on, that he was First Mate Di Chou, a bachelor.

So what if the *Chabi* sailed without him? There would be other ships. First he had to lay hands on the lovely woman with the heart-shaped face and the hank of

16

glistening hair. With her husband gone, Qing'an had nothing: no means of support but for a handful of distant, carping, unsuccessful relations. The fact that she had children was an advantage: a woman with brats has to think about how she is going to feed and clothe them. A woman with children needs a husband.

So Di Chou called on the widow to express his *sympathy* and hint that she need not struggle on alone. But it was like knocking at an empty house. Qing'an averted her eyes from his winks, his meaningful smiles, his chestful of animal charms.

No matter. Di Chou simply waited for the funeral, put on his longest face, and went along. He introduced himself to the head of the household, as a close friend of the dead Pei, willing and eager (he said) to help his friend's widow in every way he could. He had to tolerate fat Great-Uncle Bo's supercilious glances at his tattoos, his bare arms, his caulk-stained feet. But it was worth it. When Di Chou raised the subject of a marriage, he could almost hear Bo's brain clinking like an abacus. A new husband for the widow; no more drain on the family coffers; a problem solved.

'I shall give your offer my most earnest consideration,' said Great-Uncle Bo in his grandest voice.

Then the business of the rocket and the seagull and the kite intervened, and nothing was settled.

Di Chou did not panic. He knew better than to chivvy a man like Gou Bo for a quick decision. It takes a light footfall, and salt on your finger-ends, to pluck a big fat ragworm from its burrow.

Soon the relations would traipse in again from town and countryside to hear what the medium had to say about Pei's 'troubled spirit'. Before they arrived, he would speak a word in the medium's ear—persuade her to say all the right things at the seance: to say that the spirits were in

17

favour of Qing'an marrying again. Yes. That would do it. So how best (Di Chou wondered) to *persuade* the medium? With a fist, or with a fistful of coins?

'You!' said Haoyou when the medium arrived at his house for the seance. 'What happened to your face? Did someone hit you?'

'What kind of way is that to speak to your second cousin?' said his mother slapping him briskly.

He drew away. 'I only . . . I didn't know I'd met her. I thought a medium would look . . . different.'

The tall, spoon-faced, hollow-eyed girl came forward and bowed in greeting, so that her shoulder-length hair swung forwards and clashed in front of her mouth, hiding the ugly bruise on her cheek. She was friendly, polite, but her face showed a strain that had not been there at the funeral party. Her brow puckered, her mouth was a thin, straight line.

'Mipeng is your Great-Uncle Bo's sister-in-law's niece,' said his mother. 'She has kindly agreed to speak to the spirits on our behalf and ask . . . ' Her voice broke. Qing'an was not yet used to thinking of her beloved husband as an aggrieved, menacing spirit. In all her married life the spirits had never shown any interest in the little timber house hidden away in the maze of dockside alleyways.

The neighbours, intrigued as always by someone else's misfortune, crowded round the door making it difficult for the relations to push their way indoors. The straw sandals taken off at the door were quickly kicked into a muddle.

Qing'an smiled her wan little smile at each new arrival. It was all that remained of her sunny radiance, and Haoyou felt more chilled each time he saw it: that meaningless, bewildered smile, empty of joy. The medium, Haoyou noticed, wore much the same smile; her straight mouth curving up at either end like the roof ridge of a house, designed to keep demons at bay.

Qing'an began to pass around a plate of macaroons, but Great-Uncle Bo said rudely, 'Business to conduct! No time to waste!' The relations, obedient to his bullying, sat down as best they could, in a circle on the living room floor. Only Mipeng was left standing. Haoyou offered her a low stool but she only sank to the ground, as if her strength had just failed her.

'Before we begin,' said Great-Uncle Bo, his big kneecaps crackling as he folded his legs, 'I have something to say.' The family instantly fell silent. Bo pushed his big lips forward and cleaned his teeth with his tongue, savouring the power he had on such occasions as this. For the rest of the time he was a second-rank warehouseman on the waterfront, and could only bully sacks of salt and sides of pork. 'I have been approached by a man of good rank and family offering . . . ah . . . marriage to Qing'an.'

All eyes turned in amazement on Haoyou's mother, and she covered her face with one hand and lowered her head; her eyes were stretched wide with horror.

'*Mother?*' said Haoyou? 'Who?' The aunties yapped at him for speaking before he was spoken to.

'A man did call on me . . . ' said Qing'an, in a hoarse little whisper, her hand still in front of her mouth. 'A man who sailed with my husband. But I told him I had no thoughts to marry again. I sent him away.'

Great-Uncle Bo rattled his sinuses. 'A mother of children has no right to *think*. A woman with children must do the best she can for her family. *I* have thought, and I see merit in the match. We will lay it before the ancestors today . . . Then I shall speak again.' On this pompous note, he signalled with one stubby finger that the medium should begin, folded his arms across his big belly, and shut his eyes, forbidding further comment.

Haoyou was panic-stricken. Di Chou marry his mother? His whole world seemed to be sucking him down, like a pile of grain, burying him up to the waist, to the heart, to the eyes in despair. His mother marry Di Chou? Haoyou would kill him first! Tears stung behind his eyes, and he longed for the seance to be over and done, all these people gone out of his house.

Mipeng the medium clasped her ankles and rocked to and fro. Her eyes darted this way and that, truculent, mutinous, like a cornered animal. Her lids closed, her lower jaw dropped, showing small even teeth, and she began to pant and sway. The last glance she stole was towards the doorway. Haoyou turned and saw—or was he mistaken?—First Mate Di Chou watching from beyond the throng of neighbours' faces. Haoyou began to think he was being haunted—not by his father, but by the man in the leather sleeveless tunic and necklace of animal parts.

The hollows in Mipeng's throat deepened. The veins at the base of her neck began to swell and pump. Her bruised face looked as though cloud-shadow were speeding across it; her skin darkened and paled, darkened and paled. Ugly crimpings of her face made her features look as if they had been attached with clothes pegs, puckering the skin. Her top lip flapped as she breathed still more heavily. Haoyou looked away, looked around the circle of faces. He had seen faces like this before, worn by dice-players at the gaming booths.

Mipeng muttered a few words of gibberish, like a sleeper dreaming. Then her head flopped over slightly to one side. She did not look at any one person in particular, as she said, *'The spirit of Gou Pei instructs his son to be obedient to his mother and faithful to his ancestors.'*

The words struck Haoyou a blow which made his breastbone flex. The spirits were speaking to him! His own dead father was speaking to him!

'The spirit comrades of Pei say, "*Let the boy use his hands to make things of beauty. Let the boy take mastery of the wind. Let the boy make kites to sell at market. We will give him the wind in his silk. Let the boy make kites and prosper!*" '

There were a dozen murmurs of astonishment, the loudest from Haoyou himself.

'Gou Pei says also . . . ' The medium gave a convulsive shudder. 'No weddings, please. If his widow remarries, he will shower bad luck on her.' Her eyes flew open and she darted a glance towards the open door: a hunted, haunted look.

There was a communal moaning and groaning from the relations, who nodded sagely as if they could understand Pei's feelings. Great-Uncle Bo, however, scowled thunderously and jabbed his thin wife in the ribs as if trying to imply that the re-marriage had been her idea. The family looked round as if they expected Bo to speak again on the subject of the marriage. But he only rolled his big head about on his shoulders and shrugged peevishly.

Outside, there was a noise of fish racks being knocked over, and a flurry of complaints as someone pushed his way violently through the press of neighbours. Di Chou had not taken kindly the news from the spirit world.

One by one, the relations got up to go, thanking the medium, pressing coins into her hand. Mipeng herself looked limp and greenish, like a summer lettuce, and made no move to stand up herself. Soon, only she and Haoyou sat, legs crossed, opposite each other on the living room floor.

'A kite-maker? Me?' he said aloud. He did not know if he was saying it to her or to the spirit of his dead father.

'You have clever hands,' said Mipeng. Her voice was her own once again. Its ordinariness startled him.

'You heard, then?' said Haoyou, fascinated by the actual working of her magic. 'You know what the spirits said? You heard yourself talking during the trance?'

The young woman looked at him out of the side of her sloe-black eyes. And all at once, Haoyou knew. There had been no trance. She had made it all up.

'Di Chou won't be pleased,' she said. 'But he is such a . . . No one should have to marry against her wishes. And no one should have to marry a man like that.'

'Thank you,' said Haoyou, and again, 'Thank you!' He wanted to imbue the word with everything he felt: the relief, the gratitude, the pride. Single-handedly, without even the help of the spirit world, Mipeng had fought off the bestial Di Chou and turned Haoyou into a kite-maker.

'Thank you!' he said again, and just in case she thought he was simply being polite, 'Thank you! Thank you, thank you! Oh, *thank you*!'

4

The Kite-Maker

So Haoyou became a kite-maker. Haoyou the artisan. Haoyou the breadwinner. Great-Uncle Bo, obliged to obey the wishes of his dead nephew's spirit, grudgingly gave money enough to buy some lengths of reject silk, some soiled paper, sewing thread, size, and a craft knife. Haoyou went out himself to cut bamboo, which he split into spills. He made red kites and blue ones, white kites and yellow.

'Where shall I put them?' he asked his mother, holding up the first, moving his hand back and forth so that the size-wet silk breathed like a diaphragm.

'In your father's bedroom,' said Qing'an. 'I'll sleep by the hearth.' Haoyou was shocked that his model-making should oust his mother from her bed, but obedience forbade him to argue. Besides, his heart thrilled at the thought his kites were adjudged so important. Up until now, they had simply been a hobby. Now they were his profession, and his mother walked among them as through a zoo of weird and wonderful animals.

As indeed, they were.

Haoyou made triangular kites and square ones, oblongs and pennons with swallow tails. He made box kites and tubular kites, and with every one, he mastered some new deftness, learned some secret trick of quickness, and how to keep waste to the minimum.

His friends said, 'Let's see what you made, Haoyou! Let's see.' But Haoyou only smiled that polite, businessman's smile which he had seen Great-Uncle Bo use: the yes which meant no. 'When I have enough,' he told them.

His mother—quiet-spoken at the best of times—trod the house as hesitantly as a crane, and said nothing. But he heard her murmur to the family shrine, where Pei's rice bowl stood, 'Do you see, Pei? Do you see how hard our boy is working?' And then the pride and honour pricked behind Haoyou's eyes and he vowed to make the most beautiful kites Dagu had ever seen.

He made kites in the shape of fish and kites in the shape of dragons: pig faces, big rats with long tails of string. He painted them with lucky words and propitious numbers copied from over rich men's doors. He could not read himself, but he knew the importance of good luck symbols. Then, as each was finished, he carried it through to the bedroom and found a place for it among the rest. He kept the door-hanging drawn at all times, so that no one should see his stock before he was ready to show it.

'When will you start to sell them?' asked his mother, though for two months she had held her tongue.

'When I have enough,' said Haoyou, hoping to sound like his father, incontrovertible. His mother's eyes sank to the floor, but not in trusting submission, only sadness. All of Great-Uncle Bo's money had gone, and there was none left to buy rice. All the chickens had gone out of the coop. There was nothing left.

Haoyou's hand rose to cover the embroidered dog on his jacket; his palm chafed to and fro over the comforting roughness of the threads. 'When I have enough,' he said again.

His little sister, sensing that the secret bedroom was under discussion, determined then and there to see beyond the door-hanging. She hurled herself across the width of the room, ran her face and hands into the hanging, and promptly fell over. Her fall made a noise like ten dozen eggshells being broken. The hanging came adrift.

Qing'an gave a cry of dismay. Wawa had put both fists and both knees through the papery panels of a box kite in the shape of a dolphin. Like a rabbit caught in a snare, she mewed and whimpered with fright, not too young to know that she had done something utterly dreadful. With huge, miserable eyes, she looked up at her brother; the hunter whose snare she had triggered. But then her eye was caught by the sight of the bedroom transformed by Haoyou's weeks of work.

The walls were no longer visible. An undulating rainbow of colour arched overhead, and the floor had all but disappeared. His parents' bed was a mere upland in a rolling landscape of multi-coloured silk and paper.

'It doesn't matter. I can make it again,' said Haoyou, extricating Wawa from the dolphin.

His mother was staring about her. 'So many!' she said. 'I had no idea.'

Haoyou picked frantically at a knot fastening together two pieces of broken bamboo. 'When I have enough,' he said, though this time no one had actually asked the question.

In a single movement, Qing'an bent and swung Wawa up on to her hip. 'Come away, baby. Your brother is working.' And Haoyou was left standing in the doorway, looking round at what he had achieved. Hardly a space remained where he could hang another kite. The time had come to sell.

And all he could feel was gloom and dismay.

Then, who should call at the house but Mipeng. It seemed that mere chance had brought her; Haoyou did not hear his mother whisper, as she embraced the visitor, 'Thank you for coming; I didn't know who else to ask.'

Tea was fetched—the last dusty scrapings from the bottom of the caddy. Qing'an blushed with shame at the lack of rice cakes. But Mipeng did not seem even to notice. Qing'an praised her son's handiwork, and Mipeng naturally asked to see the finished kites.

Since the curtain still lay torn from its hangings, there was nothing Haoyou could do to stop her pattering demurely into his private preserve. He groaned inwardly. Now she would marvel at his cleverness and craftsmanship. Haoyou squirmed. He never knew how to answer compliments.

But all Mipeng said was, 'Do they fly?'

'Well, yes. Of course. I suppose,' said Haoyou, rather taken aback.

'You can't sell them unless they fly.'

Haoyou had been making kites ever since he was old enough to tell a bowl of glue apart from his breakfast. He was rather offended. 'If they don't fly, people can bring them back. I'll give them their money back,' he said.

Mipeng picked up a great dragony box kite with a trailing tail. 'Wouldn't it be better to test them yourself?'

'No!' He took the kite out of her hands. 'If they crashed, I'd have nothing to sell.'

'If they crash you will have no customers after the first week.' And she took the kite back out of his hand, posting it through the narrow doorway and out into the living room. 'Let's go and test this one.'

'I suppose you are waiting for the Boys' Festival,' Mipeng called over her shoulder, moving with remarkable speed, given the steepness of the hill and the unsuitability of her clothes. The hill was busy with children bundled up in six layers of tattered clothing and sent by their mothers to breathe in the wholesome air. (In point of fact, the air

26

carried oily reminders of the fish-gutting tables on the waterfront, and the wind was bitter.)

The Boys' Festival was an annual outing taken by families with thriving sons, to celebrate their good fortune and bring the boys good health and good luck. A boy with his face turned up to the sky looses all the stale vapours from his body.

He enjoys himself, too.

Haoyou had never given the Boys' Festival a thought, but he said, 'Yes, yes. That's what I thought. The Boys' Festival . . . when is it?'

Mipeng looked sidelong at him again out of those astonishing coal-black eyes. 'Next month. In the meantime, if you and your mother and sister can learn to eat air, like the dragons, all will be well.'

Above them, on the skyline, a sprinkling of kites hung in the sky like lazy hawks. The higher Haoyou climbed, the stronger the wind blew. The kite, which they were carrying between them, began to wriggle and buck, as if eager to be chasing the other, puny kites across the sky.

'Oh dear,' said Haoyou. 'I forgot the string.'

'I didn't,' said Mipeng and drew out a bobbin of cord and attached it to the dragon.

But Haoyou's legs would not take him any further. His knees were shaking. His palms were wet. 'I can't,' he said. 'Don't make me. Please.'

If he pitched his kite into the wind, he would have to watch it all over again—that hatch-cover lifting into the air, his father's hair spread out against the woven rushes, that mouth shouting out his name, the spittle like silver between taut lips, those hands and feet rigid as bird talons. 'I can't,' he said. 'Honoured father's up there.'

'So?'

Even through his fright, Haoyou was startled by this odd young woman.

'*Why did you have to say I'd make kites?*' he roared, bursting into tears. '*Why kites of all things? Father wouldn't want me to make kites! Not kites of all things!*'

The louder he shouted, the softer Mipeng spoke. 'What else can a boy with clever hands make from cheap materials? Great-Uncle Bo is not a generous man. Would you prefer I'd said your mother ought to marry the tattooed sailor?' She lifted the dragon's boxy head and appeared to be about to hurl it at him. Haoyou ducked. With a noise like a string of paper lanterns in a hurricane, the dragon swallowed the wind, reared up and thrashed into the air. The other children on the hill gave a single cry of admiration and dropped their fists, so that their kites staggered in the sky. Up went the dragon, bucking and undulating, shedding a paper scale or two from its long, fragile body. The string reeled off its bobbin with a poppety-poppety-popping. Both their heads went back: the wind was cold in Haoyou's throat. Lunging through a great figure of eight, the dragon-kite gulped in the wind and struggled skywards. One of the bamboo joints came unglued; next time Haoyou would have to use more thread to reinforce it. The tail swished. The other children on the hill gave a groan of longing. To own such a kite!

Mipeng tried to pass Haoyou the bobbin, but he snatched his hands away.

'Why? What are you afraid of?'

'Of him!' hissed Haoyou, pointing at the sky. A hilltop was no place to whisper and he had to say it again. '*Of him! He's up there!*'

'Your father?' she shouted it into the teeth of the wind. 'Well? He loved you when he was alive, didn't he? Why shouldn't he love you now?'

Haoyou's hands turned into two little fists. '*Because I let them do that to him! Because I didn't stop them! Because I didn't help him! I didn't stop them!*'

Slowly, gradually, Mipeng moved round behind him, looping her arms over his head so that the bobbin was in front of him. The circle of her arms gripped his shoulders. 'Listen. There's nothing you could have done, Haoyou. Nothing. Nothing. Di Chou wanted your father dead, because he wants your mother for himself. Nothing you could have done would have stopped him killing Pei.'

Haoyou's heart lurched into his mouth. 'How do you . . . ?'

'We've met, Di Chou and I.'

The sky spun round. Haoyou took hold of the bobbin just to keep himself from falling. He knew instantly that every word was true.

As the kite flew higher, Mipeng had to tilt her head further and further back. At last her headscarf slipped off the back of her head. And where, at the seance, there had been gleaming, shoulder-length black hair, there was nothing but a ragged tatter of stubble. She scurried after the headscarf, which was rolling across the windy grass.

He should have pretended not to see, pretended not to notice. Manners. Etiquette. He tried to fix his gaze on the kite, but out of the corner of his eye he could see her tugging the scarf back into place.

'Didn't I tell you the man was dangerous?' she said. 'He's set his heart on having Qing'an. He told me what to predict at the seance. A marriage for her. A new father for you. He didn't take it kindly when I said something different.'

Then Haoyou forgot all about the dragon tugging on his arms. A wave of hatred went through him too big for his chest to hold. He saw it as clearly as if he, and not Mipeng, was the clairvoyant. He saw that great ox of a man lurking in the alleyway, waiting his chance, stepping out of the shadows as Mipeng made her way home one night; his knife rasping at her scalp, that glory of glossy hair falling to the ground . . .

'And he hasn't given up, you know,' said Mipeng. 'He's only waiting for you to fail. You must be very careful of that one.'

The dragon-kite bounded about the sky, roaring its hatred of First Mate Di Chou, pawing the air. The other children on the hill were yelling at Haoyou now: *'Where did you get it?'*

'Did you make it?'

'How much did it cost?'

'I'm going to ask my brother to buy me one!'

'I won't fail,' he said between gritted teeth. 'I'll be the greatest kite-maker in all Dagu. In all Cathay!' He turned his face upwards towards the sky, opening his mouth wide to catch the air, just as the dragon kite was doing.

'Where did you get it?'

'How much? How much?'

'I'm going to ask my uncle to buy . . .'

'Where can we buy . . . ?'

'At my house,' Haoyou yelled back above the noise of the blustery wind. 'Plenty more like this one. Very good prices. You want to buy this one? It's for sale.'

The little boys reeled in their kites and ran home to ask their parents for money to buy a kite like the one they had seen on the hill. The dragon took longer to fetch down—it had climbed so high and resisted capture now that it had tasted freedom.

Or perhaps the spirit of Gou Pei was clutching the kite between invisible hands, examining his son's workmanship, unwilling to let go.

'How did you dare to cross Di Chou?' Haoyou asked his cousin as they walked home. 'Why didn't you just say what he told you to say? I would have.'

Mipeng's delicate, gentle face set hard like the water on a pond freezing over. 'Your honoured mother doesn't want Di Chou for a husband. No one should be forced to walk a road they don't want to walk.' There was a world of bitterness in the way she said it.

Haoyou dared one more question. 'What did the spirits *really* say to you? That day at the seance?'

But she flared up at him: fierce as any dragon. '*How should I know?*' she hissed, one hand on her headscarf. '*Tell me, eh! How should I know?*'

Haoyou ducked his head and did not venture another word all the way home.

That afternoon, they painted notices advertising Haoyou's kites: a picture of a kite, the symbol of the Boys' Festival, and an address: '*At the house of the widow Gou Qing'an.*' Unlike the rest of the Gou family, Mipeng could read and write: another surprise.

While the paint was out, Haoyou signed each one of his sixty-four kites with a little squiggling picture of a hook: the meaning of his family name. He was proud of them now. They were no longer an affront to his dead father.

'You should write Gou-Tian—Sky-Hook,' said his mother. She was smiling; the worry had gone out of her face. Even little Wawa painted symbols of her own invention, using a broken chopstick, daubing shapes on the wall with ash from the stove.

While Qing'an made soup out of cabbage leaves scavenged from under the market barrows, Haoyou ran through the warren of alleyways and lanes, wedging his notices into split-wood fences, pegging them on to washing lines, impaling them on lantern hooks:

Sky-Hook Kites. At the house of the widow Gou Qing'an. Boys' Festival soon. Buy!

* * *

31

First Mate Di Chou curled his tongue round the wad of leaves in his mouth and pressed it against his teeth. Bitter juice crawled down into his gullet, as he watched Haoyou sprint along the waterfront. From the deck of his houseboat, he could see the flutter of the notice Haoyou left on the waterside bollard, but not what it said. Besides, he could not read. In his own good time, Chou picked his way across the decks of moored ships to the quay. The notice flapped, pinioned between two turns of rope, and Chou pulled it free.

A boy was passing, laden with a pile of accounting ledgers. Chou knocked the books out of his hand and thrust the paper into the boy's face. 'What does it say?' The boy translated.

Then Di Chou raised the advertisement to his own face, spat his chew into it and screwed it into a ball. He threw it at a seagull which hopped off a few steps, blinking its yellow eyes.

Haoyou cleared the bed of kites and lay down on it, his head on the carved wooden headrest. His eyes travelled around the room trying to see his sixty-four kites as customers would see them next day. There were kite tails like girl's plaits, with bows at the end. There were tails with fireworks at the end, for use at funerals and on feast days. There were rats and monkeys and butterflies, birds and pigs and tigers. There were boxes and tubes, rectangles and rhomboids. There were faces with funny drooping moustaches. When he had sold some, and had money for fresh materials, he would experiment with fighting kites, threading blades to the strings—and noise-makers, with pieces of bamboo tube to catch the wind and whistle. Sky-Hook kites would be famous all over the province, and Kublai Khan would send for him from Dadu and want him to build great kites of jade and gold wire, and he would refuse, because the Mongols were barbarians and had stolen Cathay from the Chinese. Or there again, he might agree, naming as his price the head of First Mate Di Chou.

When he was rich, he would reward Mipeng's bravery with necklaces and silk slippers and shawls. Haoyou fell asleep at last into a turmoil of dreams peopled by flying animals and banners of black hair unfurling from the masts of a ship as it sailed through gathering black rain clouds.

The clouds were dense, choking; they swagged between the mastheads, as thick and muffling as sailcloth against his face, and they tasted of ash. The ship was sailing into the very mouth of a dragon, and the dragon was exhaling fire . . .

If the rick-rack of fireworks had not ignited, he might never have woken at all. But they went off right beside his head and he opened his eyes to find himself lying at the bottom of a whirling vortex of flame.

'FIRE! Mother! Father! Wawa! FIRE!' No answer.

The floor of the bedroom quaked and heaved, the hollow kites filling with hot air and rising like the carapace of some crumbling monster, before brushing against those already on fire and sawing this way and that in the vectors of scorching air. Round and round they spiralled, fringed like a flying carpet with tassels of fire. In burning, they drank up all the air and left nothing for Haoyou to breathe. The lining of the roof boomed with fire, melting away into embers, leaving the slates to drop, unsupported, on to the room beneath, and loosing into the sky embers which out-burned the stars beyond.

Haoyou too was a kite, burning. The bed was alight, its cover was alight, his shirt was alight. His lungs were surely alight. He listened to hear his mother screaming

33

or Wawa crying, but heard nothing. Rolling off the bed, he landed on the door-hanging still lying in a heap where Wawa had pulled it adrift. He rolled himself in it and, like some pupa grub, dragged himself into the living room, calling out to his mother and sister. Down by the floor there was a thin stratum of fresh air; the fire was dragging it in at its base. Haoyou blundered face-first into the low table, put his hands down in puddles of paint, red as blood, and on shards of paint pots and roof tiles which had cracked apart in the heat. Clumps of burning cloth blew round him, exploding pats of fire. He saw his lucky jacket folded across the stool where he had left it, snatched it to him, and found Wawa's doll underneath. Holding the doll in his teeth he crawled towards the door—out into the alleyway—where Mr Wang from next door doused him with a bucket of night-water.

Qing'an and Wawa were safe. A babble of voices hastened to tell him how a brave passer-by had rushed into the house and fetched them out—wonderful!—splendid!—a blessing on his ancestors!

Even before he looked, Haoyou knew who the stranger would prove to be.

The orange glow from the burning house made long shadows dance dementedly behind the shape of Di Chou, standing there, watching the fire, his arms still encircling mother and child, sweat glistening on his bare arms.

When she saw Haoyou, his mother ran to him and grasped his head in her hands. His teeth were clenched so tightly that it took several tugs to dislodge Wawa's doll from between them.

The whole neighbourhood stood about in their underclothes, like children at the Boys' Festival, their heads flung back, their faces turned upwards to the night sky. For rising out of the roofless building, the fragments of countless kites rode on the incandescent updraught, trailing tails of fire, lurching and plunging, climbing and ditching: a flying menagerie of flame, a fleeting festival of catastrophe.

5

Wedding

Great-Uncle Bo blamed Haoyou's dead father. He blamed Haoyou for choosing such an inflammable line of trade. He blamed Mipeng for misinterpreting the desires of the Dead. He blamed everyone except Di Chou for the burning down of the little board-built house. After all, why would a man destroy a woman's every possession and still want to marry her?

Every penny he had invested in his nephew's widow had gone up in smoke. Faced with the cost of rehousing her or, worse still, taking her in under his own roof, Uncle Bo could hardly believe his luck when Di Chou renewed his offer to marry Qing'an.

The medium Mipeng said that the spirits were against it. But if the spirits were going to be malicious anyway, what was the point in trying to stay on the right side of them?

The boy Haoyou had told all kinds of stories about Di Chou murdering his father and starting the fire, but that proved only that the boy was as much trouble as his dead father. Bo beat him soundly for his lies, and told him, 'The sooner you have a new father to beat you regularly, the better!'

Qing'an, too, was troublesome. She said she would sooner die than marry Di Chou. So Uncle Bo placed her in the care of his hatchet-faced wife, with instructions she be fed on rice and water to purge her of pride, vanity, and disobedience. True, when he saw Qing'an, perfect as a budding magnolia, standing alongside his wife Mo (lop-jawed and thin as a noodle), a strange emotion did press against Bo's heart. But the moment passed. He turned away from the beseeching sorrow in those liquid eyes and thought of what it was costing him to secure this ungrateful woman's well being. Tomorrow he would have to pay the priest, and settle the bill for the wedding breakfast. He was only lucky Di Chou was not asking for a dowry!

Di Chou lived aboard a houseboat in the harbour, and though the bride would normally be escorted, by kith and kin, to the home of her new husband, he and Di Chou had agreed the Lotus Tea House would be more commodious for a wedding breakfast than a tiny, comfortless junk. No need for fuss or expensive ceremony. After all, it was not the first time Qing'an had put on red and pinned up her hair. And Di Chou had no relations in this part of the world. Still, Bo would have to hire a sedan chair to carry the bride . . . oh, was there no end to the trouble and expense that fool Pei had caused him by dying.

Haoyou and his cousin Mipeng walked side by side through the night smells of the Dagu waterfront. Their steps made loud dents in the silence. It was ridiculously late—long past midnight—but after the beating, Haoyou had run out of the house in despair and humiliation, and Mipeng had slipped out and followed him.

They had said everything there was to say about the wrongs of it, the injustice, the unkindness. Both were in perfect agreement that tomorrow's wedding should not be happening, but there was no longer any point in saying it. Sometimes the gods are deaf.

The day before had been market day, and the waterfront was strewn with litter. Cats fed on fish-heads in front of the Lotus Tea House. They passed a sedan chair decorated with flowers—perhaps in readiness for hire by Uncle Bo next day. Inside the Lotus Tea House, the staff were rearranging furniture to accommodate the wedding guests.

'Are you ever going to marry, Mipeng?' asked Haoyou.

To his amazement she replied, 'I already have.'

Although she had never spoken about it to anyone before, the imminence of the awful marriage seemed to revive memories she had successfully crammed away until that moment.

'A marriage was made for me with a sea captain's son. Great honour. Uncle Bo couldn't believe his luck. Myself, I think it was a kind of . . . economy. The captain was a widower: he had to go away for months at a time. Me, I think he needed a babysitter for his son.'

'Why? How old was his son?' Haoyou had heard of marriages between girls of 16 and boys of 5, but only among the rich and noble, not poor families like the Gous.

'Li Ping was 20 but . . . troubled, you know?' Her eyes filled with tears. 'Troubled. By spirits. They spoke to him in his head. They told him—"Break this chair; kill that bird; hit this wife." Life with Li Ping was . . . very difficult.' Mipeng lowered her eyes, shamed by her failure to please and solace a lunatic. 'At last the voices told him to . . . destroy himself. He threw himself into Dagu dock and drowned.' Her quiet voice had sunk to a barely audible whisper. 'I sensed it. I knew what had happened. I knew him. He was always talking about the sea, dreaming about it: the voices in the sea. I told my family, "Come with me, Li Ping is dead in the water." And they came along with me. And he was. Just where I looked. Of *course* he was there! All my life I've lived here! Drowned men are *always* washed up just there. It's the current . . . But the old aunties didn't see it like that. "Look! D'you see?" they said. "Her husband's spirit called to her and she heard it. She's a medium!" That's how these things begin. All of a sudden, I was a medium.' She arched forward as she walked, bird-bony, a tuft of ragged hair escaping from under her headscarf. 'I looked inside my head, but there were no spirits. I didn't want voices in my head; I'd seen what they did to Li Ping. I tried to tell the family: *I don't want to be a medium.* When they didn't listen, I raised my voice and shouted it. "There you are, you see?" they said. "Her husband's angry spirit is speaking through her. She's a medium all right." And Uncle Bo—well, Uncle Bo heard the word "medium" and it sounded like the sweet chink of money to him. That's why it was useless arguing with him.'

Haoyou was astounded by her admission. For raising her voice to her parents, a daughter could, by law, be strangled. For speaking disrespectfully about an uncle, a person could be taken out to sea and fed to the sharks, piece by piece. Mipeng was altogether the least *proper* person he had ever met. It was only a shame that he liked her so much.

Suddenly, as Haoyou and Mipeng strolled towards a dilapidated single-storey building (known to Haoyou only as the Don't-Go-Near-House), he grabbed Mipeng's arm and pulled her into the shadows. Just going inside (at the cost of several coins handed to the doorkeeper) was the bridegroom himself: Di Chou.

Tomorrow night, this gross man in the leather sleeveless jacket, his big feet overlapping the soles of his tattered sandals, his lucky mascots jangling, would have the power of life and death over Haoyou. Tonight at least, Haoyou did not have to come face-to-face with him and be forced to speak the polite greetings which etiquette demanded. He pressed himself flat against the wall of the alleyway.

'Fine place for a bachelor party,' said Mipeng. 'You can tell what kind of friends he has.'

'What d'you mean? What is that place?'

'A drinking den,' said Mipeng, 'and such a lovely breed of customer. Drunkards come here when nowhere else will serve them. Cheap liquor fit to blind you. And it's here where half the dirty dealing in Dagu goes on. Most men, on the eve of their wedding, are honouring their relations or making offerings to their ancestors. Not Di Chou. He'd rather go drinking rot-gut with the riff-raff.' She pattered down a flight of steps, which led to the cellar beneath the Don't-Go-Near-House. Crouching down, she poked a hole in the soft, rotten wood of the unused door. When she made way for Haoyou, he was able to see into the room beyond: a cavern lit by tallow candles. Bedrolls, goatskins, and fleeces lay about on the floor, and on almost every bed sprawled a man glassy-eyed and soft-limbed with drink. Two were fighting over a pair of shoes, swinging clumsy punches at each other until they both fell over. One was singing, except that his song only had one note and no words.

Haoyou had a very dim notion of what went on inside such a place. His mother had simply given him to understand that it was dangerous and disgusting. So he was surprised to see some of his neighbours in among the lonely sailors, the waterfront thugs, and the down-and-outs with nothing left to lose. The one disturbing thing they had in common was a deathly pallor, and dark, hollow eye-sockets, as if careless thumbs had pushed their eyes too far into their skulls. They were all poisoning themselves with raw alcohol.

At that moment, indoors, Di Chou descended wooden steps into the candle-lit room. No one looked up or paid the least attention to him, except for an elderly woman who relieved him of another fistful of coins and brought him a bulging goatskin flagon of drink. Throwing himself down on the dirty palliasse, Di Chou too began to drink. There were no friends waiting for him. This was no eve-of-wedding party. Di Chou simply drank here by choice—solitary, as he set his brains awash in cheap liquor. His face showed no sign of pleasure or gratification, but his skeleton seemed to soften, so that his head sank lower between his collar bones, and the elbow on which he lay propped let him drop. At one point his head turned, and he appeared to look directly at them; Haoyou snatched his head away from the door. But Mipeng whispered, 'He's too far gone.'

And then she was climbing the steps again—and knocking on the door!

'What are you doing?!' squeaked Haoyou.

When the door opened, Mipeng took a purse from behind her belt, and said something to the doorman, who, to Haoyou's horror and alarm, allowed her to duck inside. What was going on? Was Mipeng going to confront Di Chou about his drinking? He would knock off her head! Haoyou pressed his eye to the hole in the door as hard as his nose would allow, and, sure enough, Mipeng appeared, at the head of the cellar steps, crooking a finger at the old woman in black.

A minute later, she was back outside, drawing Haoyou away down the street before his clamour and outrage could cause trouble.

'You bought him another bottle? Why? What for?'

'He'll be in a stupor now all night—probably the whole of tomorrow.'

Haoyou began to see a glimmer of hope. 'You mean, he won't make it to the wedding?'

'Right. And, if we can show the Great-Uncle Bozo what kind of a man Chou is . . .'

41

'Fetch him here, you mean? To the Don't-Go-Near-House?'

' . . . he won't let the wedding go ahead—not tomorrow, not ever.'

'Oh, Mipeng!' He wanted to hug her. He wanted to cling on tight to her, for all her outrageous disrespect, for all her unfeminine ways.

Then it came to him. It flapped into his head as darkly as his dream of the cormorant. If Di Chou had burned down one house when thwarted, what would he do when Great-Uncle Bo thwarted him yet again?

Across the harbour, the *Chabi*'s sister-ship, the *Namchi*, was noisy with activity. Even though dawn had not yet broken, its crew was making ready to sail, off-loading ballast, in the hope that it would soon be replaced by valuable cargoes. History was repeating itself. Haoyou could hardly believe how much had happened since he hurried down so eagerly to the docks with his father, to witness the *Chabi* testing the wind. If only Di Chou had sailed out of their lives aboard the *Chabi*—and foundered and drowned. But no. He had stayed on, to drink himself unconscious before seizing once and for all on Haoyou's beautiful mother.

And there dawned into Haoyou's mind an idea so black and gnawing that he thought a rat must have broken into his brain. 'Come with me,' he said, grabbing the back of Mipeng's robe. 'We're going to get him out of there and put him on his junk and cut it adrift and let him float out to sea!'

They went back to where the sedan chair stood wreathed in wedding flowers. The flowers had no colour in the pre-dawn dark. They carried the chair back to the Don't-Go-Near-House, hammered at the door, and said they had come to collect First Mate Di Chou.

'It's his wedding day!' said Haoyou to the startled doorman. 'He's due to marry my mother!'

At that, the doorman became positively helpful. He ran down the steep wooden steps on the heels of his boots, threw Di Chou across his shoulder, and reappeared carrying him. There was no doubt Di Chou had emptied the second bottle. The reek of alcohol came belching out of him in gusts as he was lowered into the sedan, and he was barely conscious, barely aware of his surroundings.

Haoyou took hold of the two poles in front, Mipeng the two behind, and they shuffled away, watched with open amusement by the doorman of the drinking den.

Haoyou thought he would die, the chair was so heavy. *'Can't . . . do . . . it,'* he grunted, and the bottom of the sedan grazed the ground, and he fell on his face. The sedan toppled forward and Di Chou slid out of it on top of Haoyou, his face clammy against Haoyou's, his mouth blowing wet bubbles that smelled of yeast.

They tussled him back inside the box-like chair—it was like trying to get a snail back inside its shell—then waddled the heavy box out of sight behind the Lotus Tea House and along an alleyway to the harbour steps. If it had not been so early, countless people would have been around to see.

Then Mipeng gave a moaning cry of anguish. *'The tide is coming in!'*

'It'll go out again, won't it?' said Haoyou pleadingly.

'Not till late morning—and how can we do it in the middle of the day? With everyone looking?'

They turned the sedan round and went back the way they had come. The weight was leaden: it made the veins stand out in Haoyou's neck and he thought his hands would come away from his wrists. Once, he dropped a pole and the chair lurched so violently that the man inside slumped over and cracked his head on the panels, moaning and cursing, but too deeply unconscious to surface.

'I know!' said Haoyou, breathless with inspiration. 'I know what to do!'

They retraced their steps to the waterfront and set down the sedan behind the *Namchi*'s piles of discharged ballast. It fell over as they tugged and wrestled Di Chou out into a heap on the ground.

The captain, a worried, fretful little man, was circulating among the various cargoes piled ready on the dock, examining the crates and barrels which might or might not be entrusted to his ship. Haoyou sensed this would not be the right person to approach. So he waited until the ship's mate appeared and started down the gangway. Then he and Mipeng hauled Di Chou to his feet between them.

'I bring my honoured father to join the crew,' Haoyou called to the mate. 'Too much celebrating.'

'You're Gou Pei's boy.'

'Thank you, yes. This is my *new* honoured father.'

The sailor looked at the groom, crumpled as a heap of washing. 'He just got married?' he said, eyeing Mipeng, as if she might be the bride, deciding she could not be Haoyou's mother.

'Yes. But he needs this voyage, sir! Spent all his money at dice. Bride no dowry, see? He's a fit man. Big man. Lots of muscles, see? A good worker. Done plenty of voyages. Needs the work.'

The mate nodded. He looked at the two eager faces: tall girl, small boy. 'Not a good time to join the ship drunk. Captain will be looking for a wind-tester shortly. He's always hard on a man who's been . . . '

'*Yes! Let him! Good!* Honoured father is honoured to be of service, sir!' Haoyou's voice chirruped with excitement. That same, nasty sensation of vicious joy stirred in his bowels. Oh, to send Di Chou aloft on his wedding day and never reel him in again!

But it was the wrong thing to say. The first mate examined him now with open suspicion, knowing there was mischief at work. 'He's no use for stowing the ship, is he? Look at him. Dead to the world.'

Two voices chorused simultaneously. *'We'll do his work!'*

It was too much for the mate. He tipped back his head and laughed out loud.

Suddenly Mipeng plucked the earrings from her ears, darted forwards and pressed them into the mate's hand. His face sobered. He looked from the fragile jewellery in his hand to the girl whose fingers had brushed his wrist. 'Please,' was all Mipeng said.

'I'll help you get him aboard.'

He picked up Di Chou as though he were a sack of beans, and carried him up the gangplank, catching the eye of the captain who hurried up the plank behind him.

'Volunteer for the wind-tester,' said the mate to the captain.

'Too big,' said the captain. 'Much too big.' He cast a chary eye at the windy sky. 'What d'you say? Is it too fitful?'

The mate, too, examined the sky, where clouds were scudding briskly overhead. He shrugged, not wanting to contradict his captain.

'Better tomorrow, maybe,' said the captain. 'I'm going to postpone. Better to lose a day than test a bad wind.' He was speaking low and furtively so that the merchants drifting now on to the quay would not hear. Postponing the wind-test might irritate them, but one bad test and they would take their cargoes away to another ship. The *Namchi* would be confined to port all season for want of good luck.

The anxious little captain was losing his nerve. The *Namchi* was not, after all, going to set sail today. Di Chou would sleep off the liquor, wake up and come looking for the people who had tried to have him shanghaied.

Haoyou crossed the gangplank in two bounds and stood in the captain's path. 'What about me?' he said.

'I don't sign the crew. See the mate,' said the captain, trying to push past.

'I'm not crew, honoured captain! I am a wind-tester . . . And it's a fine day to fly. I am a maker of kites. I know about wind. I am qualified in wind. Also my cousin the medium says it is a fine day to fly!'

The captain was astounded. He peered short-sightedly at the tall woman on the quay, who nodded vigorously. 'What are you saying, boy? That you can pull on a rope better than a dozen strong men? Get away with you, rascal.'

Haoyou shook his head till his ears rattled. 'Not *pull* on the tester, sir! Not *fly* it! Your skill is famous through all Dagu! Your experience is renowned. Not fly it, sir, no. I meant *ride* it, honoured captain. I meant ride it.'

6

Tasting the Wind

'Tomorrow,' said the captain.

'It must be today,' said Haoyou. 'Tomorrow I'll be . . . gone.'

The captain looked to the sky, looked to the merchants, arriving in numbers now on the quay, keeping brood over their cargoes of wheat, sorghum, tea, pottery, cinnamon. 'How much?' he asked. ' . . . and remember—I have sailors here who'll charge nothing for the ride.'

The words were in Haoyou's throat ready to say he would do it for nothing—just to be rid of Di Chou, just to see the *Namchi* sail over the horizon and away. But he knew he must sound plausible, professional. 'One hundred cashes,' he said. Not too little. Not too much.

'Deal!' said the captain, thinking to himself, *I wouldn't do it for a hundred tael and a kiss from the mermaids.*

The interwoven strips of bark prickled through the legs of his trousers. The embroideries on his jacket snagged. The hatch-cover which had seemed so flimsy when it cradled his father, looked now as heavy and unflyable as a butcher's tabletop.

Ropes had been forced between the slats so as to make two hempen loops which crossed at Haoyou's breastbone, and his feet, too, were tied at full stretch by the sort of intricate knots known only to sailing men. There were thongs for his hands to hold—unless, of course, he let go and clawed himself free of the harness before it could carry

47

him up . . . No! He must appear calm, as if this were his chosen profession, as if he had done it countless times before.

If the spirits favoured the vessel *Namchi* and had fair winds and calm seas in store for her, then the hatch would soar up straight above the ship. But what if the spirits knew of typhoons beyond the horizon, of sea monsters or pirates, of reefs or whirlpools? Then they would drag it out sideways, slam it into the sea, or refuse to carry it at all. What spirits? Whose spirits? Demons or cloud dragons or the souls of men who . . .

Suddenly the crew were running with him, holding him over their heads like bread on a platter, like a casualty on a stretcher, like ammunition to a cannon. He could hear them talking about him, as if he were not there:

'It's Gou Pei's boy.'

'Is he mad?'

'Sorrow enough for his poor mother, without this!'

Then they were climbing on to the raised stern-deck, and there were no more spars or sails above him—only the sky—and the wind was flexing the hatch-cover, and the men were tilting it to the vertical. He stood for a moment upright, like a man crucified, the wind full in his face. Then the hatch was lifting and he was on the underside, face-down to the after-deck, the rudder, the water, the sea, dropping astern of the ship, his soft internal organs all crammed downwards through his body and his head spinning.

Up and up the wind drew him. He had no sensation of rising—only that the world was dropping away from him. The *Namchi* was falling, the harbour falling, the ocean falling. Wind rushed past his ears in a deafening bluster. Then stillness. His stomach rose into his throat. The kite began to fall. Below him, the sailors stopped paying out rope and gave a tug.

It flexed Haoyou's spine like the cracking of a whip. A pain like a bolt of lightning went through his head and shot down the tendons of his legs. For a moment he thought it had paralysed him. But the kite caught the wind again, full in the face, and he rose smoothly now, the *Namchi* in the harbour no bigger than a pig within its sty. He could see the hugger-mugger housing of Dagu Town tumbling down towards the water's edge: the houses jostling each other like cattle at a manger. He could see Mipeng standing on the quayside, wearing her hands over her mouth. She looked like one of those Mongol women who ride into battle with scarves over their mouths. Haoyou could see the abandoned sedan chair, its flower petals blowing about on the dockside.

Haoyou was aware of a new smell. Not a smell exactly, but a lack of smells. He had risen into air unpolluted by rotting fish, sewage, and cooking, by cinnamon sacks and horse manure. Never in his life had he breathed such air! Had his father smelled this 'no-smell'? Had Pei still been alive to see the ship below him shrink to the size of a walnut in the crook of a finger, the ocean's rough surface smooth into a single sheet of shining metal? At which particular thread of this blue-woven sky had his father's body and spirit parted company?

And was his spirit here now?

Was it? Drawing him up, drawing him close, waiting to embrace him and suck the breath out of his face with a paternal kiss?

'FATHER!' he called. 'FATHER?'

Gulls, listing recklessly, dropped in and out of vision. Haoyou turned his head, to try and follow their flight, but they fled the great clumsy wooden sled skidding over the cloud vapour, invading their territory as the Mongols had invaded Cathay with their great machines of war.

49

Again the hatch-cover stalled and began to drop. Again the crew tugged on the rope, to tilt it back into the face of the wind. Haoyou's head cracked against the matting, and the rope handles burned the skin off his palms. He could hear the fibres of the rope creaking under the strain, his ribs bending inwards where the harness crossed his chest. Perhaps his kite would burst apart. Perhaps there would be no air at all to breathe at the top of the sky!

And yet such adrenalin was scorching through Haoyou that his fear seemed like someone else's—seemed to be operating outside his body. He wondered fleetingly whether his soul and body had already separated. His eyesight seemed sharper than it had ever been. The wind filled his lungs without his even breathing.

And all at once, as if fear were a cloud layer through which he had risen, Haoyou looked about him and saw the whole world beneath him. And it was his. Like a silver shield daubed with blue and green, it throbbed, convex, complex, beautiful. He was a swimmer floating on the surface of an ocean, borne up by such a clarity of water that he could see each sunken treasure, each darting fish, each twist of coral down there in the unbreathing fathoms below. He, out of all its sluggish inhabitants, could breathe! He alone had mastery over this shining province so beautiful that it spangled red and black and green in front of his eyes . . .

For a split second, Haoyou fell into unconsciousness. His muscles relaxed. The hemp slipper on his left foot slipped off—he felt it go. The speckles of colour cleared from in front of his eyes, and he saw the slipper fall—tumbling over and over, then welt-downmost, plummeting through hundreds of feet of nothingness to land in the sea.

And Haoyou's fear came back in a hot flood. Green with nausea, feeble as Wawa, frozen and feverish both at once, he knew he was trapped in the vaults of heaven like a starling in the eaves of a temple. Like a starling, it would be the panic which killed him.

'CATCH ME, DADDY!'

Now, through the rope and the woven latticework he felt a regular thud thud thudding, like a heartbeat. Was it his own terror, or the heartbeat of the Earth below him? It grew in strength, making his teeth clack together. Then he realized what it was. The crew of the *Namchi* was hauling him in—hand-over-hand—a tug-of-war team of strong-muscled men straining with all their might to fetch down the wind-tester, and singing as they hauled.

Haoyou could once more see the detail of the quayside, the merchants covering their eyes against the brightness of the sky, a barrow being wheeled along the lanes, the scorched and blackened space where, a few days before, his house had stood. Out on the greenness beyond the town, stood the Mongol tents housing the circus which he and his father had watched disembark. Over there was the warehouse where Great-Uncle Bo usually worked. Not today. Today he would be absent, dressing in his best clothes in order to marry off his niece Qing'an (or so he thought). On such days, Bo the warehouseman became patriarch and absolute master over the Gou family. Well, today Haoyou had overturned his plans. It was insolent. It was disobedient. It was heinous. But today Haoyou was a kite, a windhover riding on spread wings, and birds have no use for such words. Only when his feet touched ground would the guilt close in . . .

The familiar smells of Dagu rose up to receive him, fragrant as any rose garden. The cormorants sitting on the rocks felt his shadow pass overhead and flew away, discomforted. And Haoyou found that, indeed, some part of him *was* an expert of sorts. Though all the kites he had ever made were burned and gone, everything he had learned about kite-making was still there in his head. Di Chou had not been able to destroy that. He knew, for instance, that if he had been making the wind-tester, he would have made the ropes of the harness two different lengths, that he would have added a diagonal crosspiece for rigidity; that the square shape of the hatch was not ideal because it did not allow for the upper half of the body being heavier than the lower. He knew that his own body marred the performance of the kite and that, ideally, he should hang below it, clear of its smooth, flat, wind-catching face.

He also knew that, despite its shortcomings, his wind-tester had flown a perfect trajectory over the *Namchi*, and that the ship could now set sail crammed with cargoes for the southern ports of Shanghai and beyond. It would take along with it, Di Chou.

When the turbulent updraught from the hot town caught the wind-tester, Haoyou knew which way to swing his weight so as not to stall. He saw the faces turned up towards him, and now he could see each scar and goatee beard and goitre, each tooth missing in the gaping mouths.

A forest of arms rose up beneath him: hands and faces and shouts. It seemed like a salute, but then the hands snatched hold of his feet, ankles, knees, the frame, the harness of rope.

So perfect was his descent on to the ship's after-deck that the crew who had launched him caught him out of the very air. Then he was riding on their upraised hands, a conquering hero, a marvel, a prodigy. Everyone was jostling, laughing, shouting:

'A perfect flight!'

'Good omens, Captain!'

'Begin loading!'

'Keep that cinnamon away from the salt!'

'The gods are with you, Captain.'

'To sea on the next tide!'

Haoyou allowed himself to be untied, released from the crude, scratchy square of carpentry that had taken him up among the clouds. There were plenty of hands to help him to his feet, claps on the back, praise and admiration from three generations of men. He straightened his back, pressed the burned palms of his hands together, inclined his head in thanks, with a look on his face which said, 'It was nothing. It's all a question of kitemanship.' He braced his bruised legs—his knees did not shake at all. An exultant triumph somewhere in his chest was singing like a nightingale, and he knew that the Realm of Air was his today and whenever he chose to walk it.

Like the lava in a volcano, well-being seethed through his very core, making him taller, keeping his head erect, as the captain (merry now, and bobbing) pressed not one hundred but two hundred cashes into his hand. With kingly strides, Haoyou crossed the gangplank, and the merchants and stallholders, the snack sellers, stevedores, sedan-chair porters all burst into spontaneous applause. Children in front of the Lotus Tea House gathered up handfuls of flower petals and threw them in his face as he passed. Even the medium Mipeng joined in, twirling the sea-blue cotton of her skirt, throwing flowers which might otherwise have decorated her hair for the family wedding.

He walked on past everyone, still silent, still exultant, Mipeng falling into step behind him, Haoyou leading the way. They passed the sedan chair still lying on its side, got clear of the quay, clear of the crowds, and walked on up the narrow lanes to the top of the town. From there, they watched, in silence, the *Namchi* gorge itself on every precious cargo bound for Shanghai and beyond. As the holds filled, the mast-top dropped, but as the tide filled, the mast-top rose again, little and little, protruding further and further above the rooftops. The morning sun, still rising like a golden bubble, seemed in danger of bursting itself on the mast-tip.

At long last the *Namchi* eased, with painful slowness, away from the quay, out through the harbour mouth, riding the first ebb after full tide. Aboard it, Di Chou stirred in his alcoholic stupor. With a gentle bump, the hull against which his head rested thudded against another vessel, nosing aside his little houseboat. It toppled a bag of rice from a shelf, and sent a pack of cards cascading to the deck. Then the *Namchi* was gone from Dagu, leaving behind only the fork of its golden wake.

And only then, to his astonishment, did Haoyou's eyes overbrim with tears. He found himself leaning his face against his cousin, saying over and over again, 'Oh! Oh! I was so scared! So scared! So scared! Oh!' and sobbing as if he were a little child again and not a twelve-year-old professional wind-tester with absolute mastery of the skies.

7

The Great Miao

Great-Uncle Bo was suitably shocked by the disappearance of Qing'an's prospective bridegroom on the very day of the wedding. Di Chou had seemed so eager, so set on having her for his bride. Great-Uncle Bo shook his head in bewilderment, puffing out his cheeks in blustering outrage, as though the insult must have been aimed at him personally.

Qing'an stood, head lowered, hands joined in her lap, and the lucky coins tied to her long, curved hairpins quivered and jingled. She was dressed in her red wedding regalia—a bride jilted on the day of her marriage. Her pale, narrow face was a blank, an O, a nought.

Bo, on the other hand, could be seen cranking up the outrage he ought, as head of the household, to feel. 'Disappeared? I granted this man my permission! Disappeared? I inclined my ear to his request! It was against my better judgement, I don't mind saying. I had no wish to anger the spirits of Nephew Pei.' (He looked furtively over his shoulder at Mipeng, the medium.) 'You don't suppose the spirits have done him some harm, do you? Drowned him or some such?'

'I think he just didn't come, Uncle,' said Mipeng softly.

'*Didn't come?* Didn't come, to his own wedding? Was I holding a sword to his throat? Was I? Did I suggest a wedding? I did not! Tell me, did I?'

'Answer your great-uncle,' said Auntie Mo.

'No, Great-Uncle,' said Haoyou.

'No! And yet this fellow—this jackanape with his hairy shoulderblades and dirty fingernails—he comes to my house, eats my wife's mushroom soup, flaunts his rank at me, and asks for my nephew's widow! Bad-faced rogue. I thought so at the time. Born in the year of the snake: I recall him saying . . . As he ate my wife's mushroom soup, I might add.'

Like his mother beside him, Haoyou looked at the floor, unable to confront his uncle's blazing eyes or flying spittle.

'I've a mind to send men looking for him! My friends at the warehouse would hunt him down! A man who would take the mushroom soup out of another man's mouth!'

'You are all kindness, honoured uncle,' whispered Qing'an, 'but surely the family is lucky to escape such a man.'

Uncle Bo plucked at his shining lower lip. 'You may be right, woman. A man who drinks mushroom soup in bad faith.'

Haoyou held his breath. Safety was just within sight. The betrothal would be severed, and when Di Chou sailed back into Dagu in six months or a year, he would find the Gou family had turned its back on him as a jilter of brides and purloiner of mushroom soup.

He would vent his revenge, even so. Di Chou would be revenged on the boy and the young woman who had tricked him out of his prize. Mipeng was first to point it out, and all day long, Haoyou had been haunted by what she said. When Di Chou surfaced out of his drunken daze, asked how he came to be ten miles out at sea, the crew of the *Namchi* would tell him how Gou Pei's boy had brought him to the ship, he and a tall young woman whom he called his 'medium'. If they stayed in Dagu, Haoyou reckoned he and Mipeng had six months or a year to live.

Suddenly, there was a knock at the door. Mo went to answer it and was back in a moment, poking her beaky head into the room. With her hair newly decorated for the wedding, she looked like an apple stuck with cloves. 'Man wants you,' she hissed, her eyes irresistibly drawn to Qing'an's bridal beauty and sour with dislike.

'Me?' said the bride, the coins in her hair tinkling. Haoyou drew closer to his mother in fright. Had Di Chou woken too early and dragged himself ashore. Had the *Namchi* turned back to port?

'You? Of course not, you?' crabbed Auntie Mo. 'Is this *your* house, I might ask? Not every man wants you, Gou Qing'an. There is a man at the door to see you, husband. A *gentleman*.'

Great-Uncle Bo was flustered. Perhaps it was someone from the warehouse to tell him he should not have taken the day off for a family wedding. Perhaps a discrepancy had been found in the stores: maybe the wine he had 'borrowed' for the wedding party . . . He could almost feel the punishment rods whistling down on his ageing bones . . .

'In truth, he asked for the boy,' shrilled Auntie Mo, 'but I told him he must speak to the head of the household. That's you.'

Bo, halfway to his feet, sat down again heavily and wiped his face. 'You're a fool, woman. Have I not got better things to occupy my time on the day of a family crisis?'

'Looks *rich*,' insisted Mo in an agitated whisper.

Bo's little eyes flickered to and fro within their puffy sockets, struggling to stay abreast of events which threatened to outrun him. He rolled on his big rump, tucking the hem of his wedding robe under him, then squared his shoulders and glared at Haoyou. 'Have you been making mischief, boy? I'll beat you from here to

Dadu if you've been making mischief! Gou Qing'an! Go and change your clothes: they are too expensive to get dirty.'

Haoyou wanted to hold on to his mother—to keep her by him, but she slipped away like a slender lick of red flame, her hands already dismantling her wedding finery. Haoyou was left alone with his Great-Uncle and the man who now entered the room.

It was not Di Chou. Alongside this man, Di Chou would have looked like a tug alongside a ship. He was dressed entirely in white, except for a green silk scarf around his throat and a green leather belt around his tunic, and he carried a long white whip with a red tassel at the tip of the handle-butt. Fine, long black hair was tied back in the nape of his neck with a green cord, and his face was unblemished by disease, undented by either missing teeth or by hunger. His features were not local but marked him out as a native of some far distant province to the south.

Who was he, this handsome, elegant, clean-shaven gentleman? No distant member of the Gou family come for the wedding, that much was sure.

Bo was in two minds whether to get up and kowtow, or stay seated; whether he was head-of-the-Gou-family or a warehouseman second-class in the presence of a grandee. To be on the safe side, he got up.

Haoyou simply stared. The back of the man's silk coat was inset with picture panels of gardens and flowers and animals. And gloves! There were gloves folded over his belt-band. And shoes! He had shoes with cork heels already stained by the filth of the lanes.

'My name is Miao Jié,' said the stranger, 'otherwise known as The Great Miao, and I come in search of Gou Haoyou, the son of Gou Pei. I was told he lives here, at the house of his esteemed great-uncle.'

'What's he done?' asked Bo, eyes round with terror.

58

'He shames me daily, and I repent the day of his birth! The day of his conception, oh yes, oh yes! I hardly know the boy. I only took him into my house after his father's death.' His hands took refuge in each other, clutched close to his chest. His back crouched in abject deference.

'Then you will not grieve too much at parting with him to a good master. To an apprenticeship? An opening in the greatest trade of all?'

Uncle Bo writhed, like a stiltwalker whose stilts have sunk into mud. He wanted to change direction, but did not know how. 'What?' he snapped.

Uncle Bo knew nothing of the *Namchi* wind test, nothing of Haoyou's triumph in the skies over Dagu harbour. At one point in the telling, he even interrupted— 'No, no, sir. You have been misinformed. It was the boy's *father* who was sent up into . . . ' Then, as the full story came out, Haoyou could see him filling up with impotent rage, coming to the boil like a kettle, because no one had told him.

And yet, at the same time, a member of Bo's family had achieved renown on the waterfront. Part of Bo wanted to waddle at once to the warehouse and make certain that his comrades knew: 'That was my nephew's boy flew off the *Namchi*, you know?' As soon as this grandee in the silk coat had gone, he would beat Haoyou black and blue for making him look foolish, but in the meantime there must be some profit to be made from this, this . . . *folly*.

'Ah yes. The wind-testing escapade. I told the boy to make himself useful to the captain of the *Namchi*—a friend of mine, you know. I had not thought his little service would attract such . . . notice. It was nothing.'

The visitor smiled to himself, but if he disbelieved Bo, gave no hint of it. 'I witnessed the flight myself,' he said, 'and it put into my mind an idea for a new art, a new

59

marvel, a new way to rejoice the hearts of my public. Give your nephew into my apprenticeship, and he will take the name of Gou high into the realms of sunlight and glory!' Miao Jié's gestures seemed to fill the small room like the sword of a swaggering samurai, the long white whip mesmerizing Auntie Mo as she spied through a hole in the splitwood wall. The rice cakes she had hurried to prepare for the elegant visitor slipped to the floor off the plate, and the chickens ran indoors with high hopes.

'I am but a poor man,' Bo began whiningly. 'If his father had lived, Haoyou would have been apprenticed to the sea. And there again . . . he is so good with his hands. A kite-maker of the first quality. I had thought that his skill might keep me and my wife in our old age. Instead, you are saying I should buy him an apprenticeship, and I have to ask you, excellency, with what? What with?'

'I ask no bond money. My services are free. Do not hesitate, my esteemed Gou Bo. Give me your boy, and see the name of Gou written in the firmament: Gou Tian— Sky Hook. *"The boy who flies!"* '

Bo's mouth was open now in a foolish grin, his hands spread on his big belly as if he had been fed his own personal banquet. Miao Jié, who had been ready to offer an inducement of 500 cash, pushed his purse round to the back of his belt. A bribe would not be needed.

'What do you say, boy?' asked the visitor, turning to face Haoyou for the first time.

'What exactly . . . I mean . . . What is . . . ?'

'What *would* he say?' Bo interrupted. 'He's a lad! His duty is to his family. He'll do as he's told, never fear.'

But the Great Miao continued to look at Haoyou, thin eyebrows raised, encouraging him to speak.

'What business are you in, your honour?' said Haoyou. 'Where?'

'Why, the circus, of course, Gou Haoyou. Acrobats!

Elephants! Jugglers! Fire-eaters! And now . . . kite riders!'
He bent low, from the waist, swooping his face so close
that Haoyou could smell the rice flour whitening his face,
the fruit oil shining in his hair. 'As for "where" . . . I shall
be going upriver soon—to Dadu City!'

The wind outside made the ill-fitting wooden tiles in
the roof hop and tap and let in little whispering draughts.
His father's spirit was calling to him out of the sky, but he
could not make out the words. Was it commanding or
forbidding him to go?

'The kite . . . ' he said in a whisper. 'I would have
to build it myself. Hatch-covers weren't meant for
flying.'

Miao Jié's light brown eyes became as narrow as the
other features of his elegant face. 'In red and gold,' he
said, 'for luck.' Eyes shut, he began to conduct with his
long whip, envisaging this new addition to his circus.
'Plenty of gewgaws—streamers—and you in a costume to
match.'

'And I would need Mipeng!'

The Great Miao opened one eye suspiciously. Great-
Uncle Bo's head moved between the two, gaping with
horrified astonishment that his great-nephew should
presume to make demands of a grandee in a silk coat.

'She's my cousin—a medium. She calls to the sky
spirits for me. I can't work without her.'

The one eye closed. The whip drew small ciphers in
the air as The Miao pictured the scene—a medium calling
out to the spirits in the sky. 'I like it. Is she pretty?'

'I don't know.' (Best not bring down the gods' spite
on his cousin.) 'She's very tall.'

'She can stand in a hole. Go on.'

But Haoyou had come to the end of his terms and
conditions. He knew he was going to fly again. He had
known it ever since the first sailor's hand caught hold of

him over the stern of the *Namchi*. He had to revisit those empty lofts of the sky, go back among the birds, feel the invisible wind lift and juggle with him as it juggled with the seagulls and the clouds and the spirits of the dead.

'The circus is not a respectable trade,' said Uncle Bo, feeling himself losing control, wanting the final say in his own house, over his own dependants.

The pale brown eyes opened and Miao Jié scowled so ferociously and cracked the whip so sharply that Bo took two steps back and pulled his hands in tight against his body. 'If you want "respectable", let him go for a priest! If you want "respectable", let him sit exams for the civil service. Has he had a great many years of education, then, here in this high-smelling centre of academic excellence? There's gold to be milked from the sun, Gou Bo, and your great-nephew can milk it. Is he mine?'

'He's yours,' said Great-Uncle Bo.

Auntie Mo limped into the room, little hands, little feet, long body. She offered a tray of rice cakes to The Miao, one with chicken feathers sticking to it. With an elegant bow, The Miao declined the offer of refreshment. He had an evening performance to oversee, he said.

The Jade Circus was an odd mixture of opposites. Parts were more putrid than the foulest corners of the fish market, and parts were glimpses into the fabled City of Gems. Elephants like drought-dead trees stood amid steaming piles of dung, and stocky little horses with hogged manes ate out of crates of sweepings from the market. A red panda sat listlessly scratching itself, and two camels, legs folded under them, spat at anyone who passed by. There were pyramid piles of bird cages, each with a different songbird inside, snared specifically so that they could be freed at the end of each show.

And there again, there were boys in cloth of gold, dancers in saffron-coloured silk and with bells on their fingertips. There were stilt-walkers with trouser legs a boy could never grow into: their kneecaps started above Haoyou's head. There was a woman in a blue veil, standing on the saddle of a white pony.

'My best riders are Mongols,' Miao Jié explained. 'Steppes men and women. Born in the saddle. Scared of nothing but the gods and lightning.'

Mongol yurts stood around—tents like giant patchwork cows—bits of hide stitched together and propped up with a skeleton of strong tent poles (and a smell just as strong).

There again, there were brightly dressed people climbing up each other like flowers vying for the light, balancing on shoulders, heads up-stretched, hands upheld. There were musicians blaring on their tinny instruments, and a girl with a ribbon on a stick making it whirl into a single rolling circle.

'It's perfectly true, what your relation says,' said Miao Jié, resting a hand on Haoyou's shoulder as they walked. 'Ten, twenty years ago, show people like this were nothing but talented beggars scrabbling in the dirt for the coppers people threw at them. But these are new times, Qiqi. New times. The Newcomers love a circus. They can appreciate feats of daring: thrills and skills.'

'The Mongols, you mean?' said Haoyou, shocked to hear anyone speak of them without a sneer and a spit.

'The Northerners, yes. Our conquerors. Our rulers. Our new royalty. One day, Qiqi, you shall perform in front of The Mighty Khan himself—Kublai Khan, Emperor of all Cathay. What do you say to that?'

Haoyou gave this some thought. 'I say my Great-Uncle Bo would sooner cut me up and burn me for firewood. He says all Mongols are murderers and barbarians.'

Miao Jié threw back his head and laughed a theatrical laugh. 'Ah well. You have nothing to fear from your Great-Uncle Bo. You are under my protection now. It's for *me* to cut you up and burn you for firewood if you disappoint me.' And he laughed again.

But Haoyou shuddered, as if a clammy hand had just drummed its fingers between his shoulderblades.

There were squat-down, smoke-in-your-eyes primitive little cooking fires where old women crouched cooking food for sale to the audiences. There was a conjuror cramming things into the recesses of his mouth—coins and ribbons and paper money. There was a dragon mask lying legless on its side in the dirt, its big goggly eyes squinting at the camels. A juggler. A strong man. A caged tiger and jaguar. A singer.

And Mipeng. Tall and leaning, like a weary heron, she stood beside the cloth bag which contained her worldly belongings. Eyes fixed on a pile of horse manure, her face expressed nothing. The various shocks in her life had wiped her face clean of tell-tale expression. But she gave off an aura of unease as powerful as the tiger in its cage.

'I'm sorry,' said Haoyou, when they were alone together. 'I couldn't think what else to do. Di Chou is sure to come looking for us when the *Namchi* comes home. What could I do? He'll know it was me. He'll know it was us. 'Sides . . . you said you never wanted to be a medium. Didn't you?'

Mipeng looked around her, a look which asked wordlessly if the Jade Circus was really a better option.

'I suppose Great-Uncle Bo is angry with me for taking you away,' said Haoyou. 'No more fees from your work with the spirits.'

She gave a great sigh. 'Uncle Bo is always angry. I think he learned young that it was easier than listening.'

She subsided onto her bundle of belongings. Haoyou was aghast at what he had done to her.

'Go home if you'd rather,' he said helplessly.

Mipeng shook her head. A frown shaped like a seagull settled between her eyes. 'No,' she said. 'No. I'll stay until you kill yourself, Gou Haoyou. Then I'll go home and comfort your mother.'

8

Qiqi

Qiqi.

It meant 'Up-in-the-Air', and the citizens of Dagu had never seen the like. The fact that the performance could only take place on windy days did not lessen Qiqi's value to the Jade Circus. For people came to the circus to see the flying boy and, if they were not able to see him, came again to salve their disappointment.

Haoyou built the kite frame out of young bamboo, the cladding out of heavyweight paper, coarse with shreds of rag and wood and pith. He and Mipeng painted it scarlet, and crammed each red panel with golden writing. To him, they were mysterious, mystical signs—many-legged insects crawling over a crimson mountain. But Mipeng read them aloud as she worked: 'crane', 'luck', 'sunrise', 'fortune', 'happiness', 'dragon', 'songbird', 'mountaintop', 'phoenix'. He was astounded that she—a member of the humble and ignorant Gou family, could read and write, but did not dare to ask her how or why she could. He practised secretly, writing the magical symbols and numbers in the dust with a stick.

Mipeng combed the tails of the circus horses for strands of horsehair which she dyed and stitched to the tail end of the kite as it hung in the branches of a tree. When they stood back to admire it, it seemed as though the tree were holding out the kite to them: *Look, isn't it fine?*

It was. A scale flicked from a crimson dragon, the shield of a giant warrior, the rearing, diamond head of a scarlet snake. The fact that the sight of it unstoppered in

66

Haoyou a fountain of incandescent fear only increased the magic of the thing in the tree.

Fortunately, the hot crescent of Dagu bay could usually be relied on to drag in a strong, cool, evening wind off the sea, and for a long, lilac hour created a thermal ladder up which Haoyou would climb to the clouds.

'And now your costume, Qiqi!' said the Great Miao after a few days. A Mongol woman, burned almost black by sun and snow, held up a crimson suit of clothes: tunic and trousers in raw red silk with tinkling gilt bells attached, and a red felt cap. Haoyou was entranced. The Miao waved a hand and the woman began to tug on the sleeve of Haoyou's cotton jacket.

At once, he pulled free of her and clasped the jacket close across his chest. It was too small for the edges any longer to meet. 'It's cold up there,' he said. 'Silk won't keep me warm.'

'There speaks a boy who has never worn silk,' said the Miao. 'Silk is warm in the cold and cool in heat.'

'Not up there!' Haoyou pulled free again, fists tightly clenched around his ragged revers. 'I'll wear it over the top.'

But with the tunic over his wadding jacket, he looked like a fat little emperor. The Miao would brook no argument; he signalled to the woman with a nod of his head, and the woman wrestled Haoyou out of his old faded jacket. She was stronger than his father had ever been. 'We cannot have our phoenix smelling of fish and bad drains,' the Miao said, biting off the words sharply with his perfect white teeth.

A band of trees on a nearby hill began to move uneasily. Rain spat as the tide turned. The evening wind was rising. The Miao whirled his whip to stir his artistes into action. 'Quickly now! Our public is waiting!'

The little wadding jacket lay on the ground, kicked this

way and that by running feet. One of the elephants trod on it on its way to the flat waste ground where the evening performances took place. Two roustabouts lifted the kite out of its tree and began toiling uphill with it to the space between the restless trees, from which Haoyou would take off. The huge red diamond flexed over their two heads, like a butterfly drying wet wings. The new horsehair tail splashed itself across their backs.

Haoyou trailed after them, his costume flapping round him more violently the higher he climbed. It was a strong, steady wind, perfect by any standard. And yet Haoyou knew he was going to die. He knew that the kite was going to slam him into a tree or a boulder, or drop him among the elephants to be trampled. He knew that his father's spirit, armed with its fishing rod, would play him like a red snapper, and then throw him back into the sea.

Below, on the waste land, in an arena cordoned off from noisy pushing spectators, acrobats were somersaulting, leap frogging, cartwheeling their way through the tarry smoke of torchlight (although the sky was still blue). A Mongol warrior was pitching curved short-swords at a girl in a demon's mask, while riding around the arena at breakneck speed. Haoyou could hear the drum of the hooves.

The roustabouts had uncoiled the rope—a phenomenally long splicing together of ropes—and were waiting to lash him to the kite. He could feel the hoofbeats now, vibrating through his back as he lay down on the wooden cross-pieces, face-up to the sky. He would not make difficulties for them . . . but he knew it would all go wrong, even so. His luck was gone. It lay trampled under the blunt, stumpy feet of the elephants, shredded by the passing hooves of Tartar horses. Cold against his skin, the red silk costume was a chilly, flapping shroud, but politeness and duty forbade him to say so. The brass collar his mother had put round his neck was supposed to fool the gods into thinking he was a dog and not worth picking on, but the gods can't be fooled that easily. Haoyou knew about dogs, knew that he was no longer protected from misfortune now that his Little Dog Wu was gone.

Jabbering at him in a language he did not understand, the Tartar roustabouts raised him upright. The wind immediately butted him in the face, shook the kite, pierced the fibres of his red finery.

'Wait!'

Mipeng was labouring up the hill, her long tunic gathered in one fist, her feet scuffing pebbles out of their sockets in the side of the hill. She discarded her shoes and pressed on in bare feet. *'Wait!'*

The roustabouts, deafened by the thunderous rattle of the kite, continued their work. They threw Haoyou upwards, and ran to pick up the rope. Mistiming it, they failed to catch the wind, and the frame barged its pointed tail back into the hillside; the jolt bit into Haoyou's back like a dog bite. Then, just as the roustabouts lifted him upright again, Mipeng reached her cousin and pressed something into the palm of his tethered hand. He felt it—a rag of torn cloth rough with embroidery. It was Wu. She had torn it off the old jacket and brought it to him: Little Dog Wu.

Haoyou closed his fist and laughed out loud—a laugh like a great sob. He kept his fist tight closed all through that flight. The little red cap slipped off his head and spun to earth like a drop of blood nicked from the sky. The spectators below gave a gasp and followed its progress downwards until it fell behind the hill. But Haoyou kept tight hold of Wu. The crowds were nothing but faces—a clutch of white eggs resting on a shapeless nest of green. But the noise of their amazement came up to him, their gasps of 'Look!', and 'Aaaah!'

69

The little children seated on their fathers' shoulders tugged at ears and hair and nose, saying that they too wanted to fly. The evening sun shining into Dagu windows flashed on metal pans and lamps, making the city glimmer. A finger of red cloud out over the sea pointed to Qiqi Up-in-the-Air, and the trees on the hill nodded enthusiastically as if to say, 'We know. We see. We are acquainted with him.' Inside Haoyou's palm, Little Dog Wu lay curled up, cold and crisp and familiar. The feeling was so much part of his babyhood that Haoyou's thumb might have strayed into his mouth but for the ropes tethering his wrists.

He felt no pain from the rope burns, felt only the acrid simmer of terror and glee tucked in under his ribcage like a lit lamp. He could not understand why the rope-men fetched him down so soon. After a few minutes airborne? Why not give the public their money's worth? But no. The luminous bay and the jaws of Dagu harbour resolved themselves into a legible map, then into particular buildings, and then he was over the hilltop again, the trees reaching for his legs as the sailors aboard the *Namchi* had reached up to catch him.

He landed in soft, long grass so dark with evening that the daisies floated like lotus blossoms on a pool. How suddenly night had come down, thought Haoyou.

Pushing through the grass came a small spotted pony ridden by a Mongol. Then Haoyou was up on the Mongol saddle-bow, being led downhill to the arena. The crowds parted to make way for him. The Great Miao stood at the heart of the arena, white whip upraised to present him: '*I give you the Bird Boy: Qiqi!*'

But among all the staring faces, Haoyou saw only his mother's. Eyes full of reproach, beautiful mouth set in a desolate downward curve, she fixed him for a moment with a look so accusing that he might have committed

70

murder. Then she turned deliberately away, and disappeared into the crowd.

The Great Miao told him he had been in the sky not five minutes but half an hour. It proved still more convincingly to Haoyou that the sky was a different country, where even Time passed at a different pace. 'I like the crowing noise,' Miao added. 'The crowing noise was good. It echoed nicely off the hill. Keep in the crowing.'

'Crowing?' said Haoyou, unaware of having even opened his mouth let alone given vent to a cry of delight at finding Little Dog Wu once more.

That night, as Mipeng sat sewing Dog Wu on to the lapel of the scarlet tunic, raucous laughter and shouting floated across from the Mongol encampment. The Tartars were drinking koumiss—fermented mare's milk—and since they always drank first and ate afterwards, it was not long before they were all ferociously drunk. A brawl broke out which rolled in among the hobbled horses and between the yurts, gathering more and more men into it, like a snowball gathering snow. Cooking pots clashed, a collection of banners fell with a rattle. A man squatting down, with his trousers round his knees, was knocked over and embroiled in the fight. The elephants half rose, scenting the agitation with upraised trunks. Then the scrimmage of men rolled into the mouth of a yurt and snapped the centre prop, fetching the whole heavy tent down on top of them. Women's voices swelled the noise with shrieks of temper.

The Great Miao ducked out of his own tent and stood watching, his immaculate clothing still as pristine as when he had put them on in the morning. He appeared to value his scrupulous cleanliness too much to approach the dirty mêlée of squabbling Mongols, for he watched from a distance, standing as erect as the white whip which never left his hand.

'Barbarians, aren't they?' said Haoyou loudly. 'Great-Uncle Bo said: they're all barbarians who do their toilet in public.'

The white whipcord cracked an inch in front of his nose.

'Well, they're your kinfolk now, *Emperor* Qiqi,' said the Miao. 'In a circus, every man is kin to every other. For your information, these, your brethren, are nomads, born in the saddle. It irks them to stay too long in one place. They've had enough of Dagu. And so have I. It's time to move on.'

'Leave Dagu?'

It was hardly unexpected. Haoyou had known all along that the Jade Circus would leave. Indeed, it had to, if he and Mipeng were to escape the wrath of Di Chou when he sailed back into port. But in all his life, Haoyou had never known anywhere other than the Dagu waterfront, its smells, its people, its markets, its spirits, its backdrop of hills.

'You are what the Mongols call a *tajik*,' said Miao Jié. 'A city-dweller. A keeper-to-one-place. You should venture further afield. Here, whatever I call you, you will only ever be Gou Haoyou. Somewhere else—who knows?' He stepped up behind Mipeng and bent in an elegant curve, like an archer's bow, to see what she was sewing. (Haoyou noticed how she drew herself inwards as Miao's long, gloved hand reached down and smoothed the worn old patch of Little Dog Wu.)

Haoyou felt found-out, ashamed, childish. 'I need it,' he said lamely. 'For luck.'

But The Great Miao did not laugh, did not tell Mipeng to unstitch it. He said, 'We all of us need luck, Qiqi. Luck has played a great part in my own life. I understand about luck. I pray your dog will always bring you the luck you deserve. Get to bed now. Tomorrow we shift ground.'

'Where are we going?'

'Upriver to Dadu, and wherever else the river takes us. Go to bed, *tajik*. You're a barbarian now, and barbarians like nothing to do with the dark.'

The cousins lay on their bedrolls, their outdoor clothing standing guard over them in the darkness, hanging from the tent poles of a cloth tent, and listened to Mongol warriors crawling about on hands and knees looking for their bracelets, drinking cups, shoes, teeth. Intermittently the drunkards were sick amid the elephant dung.

'You're afraid of him,' said Haoyou. 'You are, too, aren't you?'

No answer.

'Why is that? Can you see something coming? In the future?' (Still he could not quite rid himself of the idea that Mipeng was a medium, endowed with magical insight.)

'I hope not,' said her voice in the darkness.

Now what kind of an answer was that? Haoyou got up, took down his new tunic and laid it beside his bed, lapels outermost, so that he could sleep with his hand on Little Dog Wu.

9

Translation for Beginners

Haoyou's mother would not even bid him goodbye. She turned her face to the wall when he entered the house, and no amount of pleading would make her turn back to face him.

'I can do it!' he pleaded. 'I'm good with kites! You know I am!'

Qing'an put her fingers in her ears.

'I'll come home rich!' said Haoyou in desperation. 'Richer than Great-Uncle Bo! I'll come home with enough money to build us a new little house, just like before!!' But Qing'an only leaned her face into the corner of the room and signalled sharply with her hand for him to go, go away.

Wawa, entering the room and seeing her brother, came running over, arms outstretched. 'Qiqi! Up-in-the-Air!' Their mother gave an inarticulate roar, swept up Wawa into her arms and fled the room. Haoyou had no choice but to leave the house and rejoin the long queue of bullock carts bearing the Jade Circus down to the river.

As he turned his back on the house, something struck him on the shoulder. Looking behind him he saw, in the road, a bone. His mother had thrown an old meat bone at him—him who had saved her from marriage to Di Chou, him who had brought her morning tea for five years and asked after her health every morning since he could speak.

Mipeng, already aboard one of the carts, sitting in the little angle of space left by the gigantic scarlet kite, reached out a hand and helped him over the backboard. 'How is your honoured mother?' she asked.

Haoyou pitched the bone out on to the roadway, and a pack of stray dogs raced out of the alleyways to fight over it. 'She threw that at me!' His voice came out shrill and tearful, so he did not go on. When Mipeng smiled, he wanted to hit her. *'It's not funny!'*

Mipeng folded her long body into the corner of the cart and went back to reaming holes in the sides of short bamboo sticks, using a pointed knife. 'Don't you understand? It was only to fool the gods. To make them mistake you for a dog. They won't trouble with a dog, but you . . . her boy. Her dear boy.'

Haoyou did not answer, but the words reached inside his ear like the corner of his mother's apron on bath night, and he did not argue, because he so much wanted them to be true.

In Dagu he was Qiqi. But as the Jade Circus travelled north, he changed name with every new venue: Cheng Xia, Ride-the-evening-cloud; Teng Tian, Soar-in-the-sky; Ying, the Fly.

The little stems of holed bamboo, strung beneath the kite, caught the wind and made a weird, unearthly whistle. The Great Miao was delighted and congratulated Mipeng on her inventiveness.

'It is time for your honoured cousin to show herself,' he said one day, and Mipeng, who was busy shaving Haoyou's head, started, and nicked his scalp. 'Me?'

'Qiqi says that you summon his father's spirit. I ask only that you do it in the arena, where the people can see you.'

'But I . . . ' Surely she wouldn't deny it? After all, the Jade Circus fed and housed her, on the strength of her mystical powers. Haoyou held his breath. Mipeng's eyes sank to her shoes. 'It is not in my nature to . . . to draw attention to myself.'

The Miao said no more, but within two days a costume appeared on the wall of their little tent—scarlet and gold, with a veil such as the Mongol women wore. Costumes were the single most expensive investment the circus made. They were not gifted lightly to the 'extended family' of the performers. It was plain Miao Jié was not going to let her refuse.

'Put it on,' said Haoyou, dazzled by the glittering magnificence of the robe.

'I don't want to summon the spirits,' she said, jutting her little pointed chin, her spoon-shaped face.

'Put it on anyway. Just to show,' he wheedled.

'I said I don't *want* to summon the spirits.' She clenched her hands into fists.

'You'd only be pretending!' Haoyou pulled the costume down from where it hung, holding it out for her to put on, like a coat, over her existing clothes.

She clenched her teeth—an adult suddenly, losing patience with a child. 'Just suppose they came!' she muttered through gritted teeth. *'Suppose the spirits came when I called.'* And she retreated into the tent, her red silk crushed between her hands.

When Miao Jié came sauntering by, walking with the long lope of a lord walking his estates, Haoyou was worried. What would happen if Mipeng defied him? Would he take the white whip to her? Or turn her away from the circus in the middle of nowhere, alone and unprotected and miles from home?

Happily, just then, Mipeng ducked out of the tent . . . and she was wearing the red robe! Her short hair was hidden by a pretty scarf, and she had plaited the remains of the red horsehair into bracelets which ringed both arms. Nervy as a roe deer, she stood not face-front seeking his approval, but side-on to the circus master, her eyes on the middle-distance.

'What does your cousin think of the omens for the evening?' Miao Jié asked Haoyou. 'Perhaps she can ask the spirits.'

Haoyou felt awkward. He felt oddly in the way, like an interpreter between two foreigners.

'It's not steady like the wind off the sea was,' Mipeng observed. 'Gou Pei's spirit belongs in Dagu. There is a chance he may not come, even for calling.' She said it to Haoyou, but it was directed at Miao. Haoyou gulped.

'Then perhaps your cousin could ask the local spirits to do their part,' said Miao Jié to Haoyou, and moved off, like a reed floating downstream.

'I'm sorry you hate him so much,' said Haoyou, feeling responsible for his cousin's plight.

She shot him a glance so violent that it all but knocked him over.

'Sometimes, cousin, you are twelve kinds of a fool,' she said.

The Jade Circus acquired a small flotilla of barges, which the elephants were to tow up the length of the Hai River. The Mongol riders were deeply suspicious of boats, and kept to the bank, fretful and scowling. Sometimes they would disappear for two and three days at a time, without explanation. It was Haoyou's opinion that they went off to murder someone and cut off their head. 'They love to cut off heads,' he said, quoting his Uncle Bo. They had pouchy, leathery cheeks slung across the bridges of their noses, like saddle bags, and their eyes were small, winged by deep creases where they had ridden through blinding white winters and blazing desert days. Their idea of a beautiful woman was one with a single black eyebrow beetling beneath her blue headscarf, and they did indeed relieve themselves in public. Wherever Haoyou looked, mornings and evenings, he saw sights which made him look quickly away, only to be confronted by a goat being slaughtered or a carcass being flayed. The Mongols treated with contempt the Chinese acrobats, slight and lithe and almost girlish in their delicate nimbleness—but Haoyou they treated with superstitious awe. For he ventured into the realm of lightning, and lightning terrified them more than any danger or hardship.

Unfortunately, because they were on the bank, the Mongols were first to arrive in each town along the river. It was not good for trade.

At Yangcun, the Miao summoned all the children together—the juggler's twin boys, the magician's pretty daughter, the rabble of Mongol children born under a variety of skies—and told them to run through the town shouting out that the Circus had arrived.

Gradually figures emerged, wary, suspicious. These were not seaport residents accustomed to seeing all nationalities and new novelties every day. They stared at the pyramid of acrobats with blank bewilderment, as if to say, 'What are they doing? What is it for?' The conjuror was greeted with murmurs of 'Demon!' When the trick riders appeared, the audience reached for their young and made as if to take them safe home. Here were people who still felt nothing but dread for the Mongol race which had conquered their country.

The Great Miao strode to the centre of the square, signalled for the riders to withdraw, and raised his voice in an announcement. 'I bring you now Sun Swallow, who rides the wind, who soars with the birds, who can travel in among the spirits of your ancestors!'

Still the crowd was silent, but now it was a new kind of silence, stunned and watchful. The kite was hurried into position: with every minute that passed more of the crowd peeled away, like sheep straying. Nothing produced by these strangers off the river could have any relevance to the insular little lives of Yangcun.

The wind was fretful and blustery—a swirl of captive air tossed between the bumpy hills, squeezed by the river canyon. Haoyou had to look to the clouds to know which way the higher winds were blowing.

The roustabouts threw him into the air like a ball tossed up to amuse a grizzling, listless baby and, like a baby, the crowd was suddenly enthralled. They did not grin or break into applause. Their faces were serious. As they looked up, dozens of caps fell to the ground unnoticed. The Great Miao breathed a discreet sigh of relief.

The turbulence was fearful—a torrent of wind flowing seawards, like the river below. The horsehair thrashed up between his legs; something unfamiliar and hard rattled round his ankles and he felt sure the whole kite would stall and drop out of the sky. The lining of his stomach appeared to be screaming, and it was a long time before Haoyou realized that the noise came from the bamboo howlers Mipeng had attached.

Playing on the hill behind his home town, he had heard plenty of kites whistle and peep, but he had never realized how loud the noise was, close up: a desolate, ghostly howling which seemed to echo off the dome of the sky, a dismal, mournful, supernatural noise.

The people on the ground heard it. Unlike Haoyou they had never strung sound devices from their kites, and the noise was new to them. They listened, heads up, hands straying to the lucky charms round their necks. They thought they were hearing the voices of their ancestors.

When, two hundred feet above them, the kite boy was sick, they thought they were seeing the spleen of their ancestors take on material shape and drop in among them with a splash.

Nauseous and miserable as he was, 'Sun Swallow'

saw, as the rope-men reeled him in, that something odd was happening far below him. The crowd, instead of staying in the Miao's chosen show site, were all running towards the hill, surging around the rope-men, snatching at the rope. Were they angry with him for being sick on their heads? They were all shouting, faces jostling as close as frogspawn, every mouth open. He struggled to separate words from the general hubbub:

'Did you see my mother?'

'Did Great-Grandfather Xian give you a message?'

'Was Ming Ti Chep there? A big angry man with green teeth?'

'Were my babies there?'

Finally the spectators caught Haoyou out of the air with reverent hands, convinced still further by his white face and stained clothes that he had been among the spirits. They pressed round him in such numbers that none of the circus hands could reach him to cut him free, and he remained spread-eagled on his back, pinned down by hysterical peasants and shopkeepers, their spit wet in his face as they shouted.

'You spoke to my father?'

'Is my husband still angry with me?'

A foot went through one of the kite's fragile panels.

'Did Hop Li Yung poison my chickens?'

'Who did Chang want to inherit the business?'

Then the white whip cracked. The people stood stock still, eyes wide, their clamour silenced. 'If you would be answered, let "Sun Swallow" speak!' declared Miao, in the tones of an emperor.

But 'Sun Swallow' did not speak. 'Sun Swallow' had nothing to say. He opened his mouth but all that came out was, 'I'm sorry, I—'

What was he supposed to say? He had seen no spirits, spoken with no spirits. They were invisible, higher up or hiding. Perhaps they scattered like fishes when the great red shark came swimming into their habitat. What was he supposed to say? He looked to the Miao for help, but the only clue was a quick frown urging him to say something, anything. What was he *supposed to say*?

'The spirits speak a language all their own!' A high imperious voice cut through the charged atmosphere.

'Did you not hear them? The dialect of Heaven is not the dialect of Earth. My messenger does not speak the tongue of the spirits. But I, Tongue of Fire, will translate for you!'

It was Mipeng, speaking from the crest of the hill, her figure a silhouette against the sky. 'Come hither, "Sun Swallow", and tell me what you heard!'

Haoyou scrambled free of the kite and up the slope to join her, hampered by the feeling that the ground was moving under his feet. Panic-stricken, he stood on tiptoe to whisper in her ear: '*I didn't hear anything!*'

'The ancestors of this place rejoice in their children, and their children's children!' Mipeng's voice came out so loud that Haoyou almost jumped out of his wits.

'*But there wasn't anyone there!*' he whispered desperately.

'They say: Make time for happiness!' boomed Mipeng.

'*I think I drove them off!*' hissed Haoyou in her ear.

'They say that a time of great peace is coming . . . but that there is danger in the river.'

'*I was sick!*'

'Beware of floods!' Mipeng announced.

Haoyou kept his nose stuck into the side of his cousin's hair—it was comforting, even though he could not think of anything else to whisper.

That did not stop Mipeng loudly translating for the benefit of the crowd.

' "Remember the stories you were told as children! Keep the Festival of Boys. Honour the gods with a thousand lanterns, and do not drink from impure waters!'' These are the words of your ancestors.'

The crowd stared. The crowds made *kowtow* to the medium and her winged courier. It fell back, too overwhelmed and too astonished to remain a mob, resolving into thoughtful, nodding individuals, happiness spattering their faces like porridge thrown by a baby.

The acrobats began their tumbling tricks. The musicians began to play. The beast-handlers contemplated bringing the elephants up from the river bank. But the people of Yangcun were not interested in thrills and marvels. They had just established contact with their ancestors, and it would take more than elephants to budge such a thought from their minds.

'How did you know, cousin?' said Haoyou, as they sat in the boat later, pasting paper over the tears in the kite.

'Know what?'

'Know what their ancestors wanted to say. I didn't tell you. I didn't know. I thought you said you weren't a medium. I thought you said . . . '

Mipeng looked at him with her head on one side, and an odd expression on her spoon-shaped face. 'Oh, Haoyou. Be glad the gods gave you the gift of clever hands,' she said. 'They certainly held back on the brains.'

Miao Jié had decided to cast off from Yangcun and continue on upriver. Pleased as he was with Mipeng for defusing a dangerous situation, he could not see how any money was to be earned from a community so frowsy and sober that they saw no point in entertainment. Even The Great Miao was capable of miscalculating.

The circus folk were woken by the squelch of a hundred pairs of feet in the riverside mud, beyond the bulkheads of the barges. It sounded as if a herd of cows had come

82

down to drink, but when Haoyou poked his nose above the rail, he saw that the whole town of Yangcun had turned out in force: a deputation of householders, shopkeepers, widows, craftsmen, and farmers. The caged animals set up an agitated racket, rushing up and down their cages. The Mongols, encamped on the bank, came to the doors of their yurts hand-on-sword.

'What do you want?' For the first time, Haoyou saw The Great Miao dishevelled, his long hair hanging loose, his feet bare. But he held his white whip, even so, and had the air of an animal trainer confronting a rogue tiger.

'Sun Swallow and Tongue of Fire!' called the people on the bank.

Haoyou and Mipeng crawled under a tarpaulin and held the edge down hard against the deck with knee and elbow and hand. 'We should creep down closer to the elephants,' breathed Mipeng. 'People never dare go near the elephants.'

'I know,' hissed Haoyou in reply. 'I'm one of them.'

'We have messages!' called the people on the bank. *'We need Sun Swallow and Tongue of Fire!'*

And suddenly The Miao recovered himself. The people puddling and squelching in the mud were not angry after all, but eager, urgent, pleading. Above all, they were willing to pay now for the services of Sun Swallow. They were in no mood to be turned down, but they had not come to lynch anybody. On the contrary, they would not have laid a finger on the medium who spoke the language of the spirit world, nor on the courier who was about to deliver their prayers in person to the celestial ancestors.

They stood holding out flowers and sachets of spices, biscuits, and paper money. Some, who could write, or afford the services of a scribe, were holding out fluttering strips of paper with messages on them.

They had locks of their children's hair, wads of tobacco, and little paper models such as Haoyou had made for his own father's funeral. It was as though a ship were setting sail for some remote, inaccessible land and suddenly the people saw a chance to send gifts and letters to family members who, until that moment, had seemed too far away to be contacted.

'There's no wind! It's not good weather!' Haoyou protested as The Miao hurried him into his costume.

'Do your best, boy. You needn't go high.'

'But it's the wrong time of day! I never flew in the morning before—not since Dagu!'

Unfortunately, the people of Yangcun were not interested in weather patterns or the science of flight. What they had seen the day before had not been a stunt to them, but magic, and a most useful kind of magic, at that. No sooner did Haoyou appear in his red costume, and step ashore, than they pressed forwards and began pushing their hands inside his clothing, stuffing him with gifts and messages for their ancestors. They shouted names in his ear, told him how to recognize their kin. They tore his red silk, pinned notes to his trouser legs, wedged chopsticks into his boots. Someone even pushed a cloth bag of green tea into his mouth.

'They'll stuff him like a chicken,' said Mipeng in a low voice. The Miao glanced down at the unaccustomed feel of a hand clasping his. He did not seem to comprehend the danger. Mipeng persisted: 'The kite is built to carry only Haoyou—not Haoyou stuffed!'

The slight rocking of his head showed that the Miao had grasped the problem. 'Tell Dakhur to fetch out the birds. The bird-catcher, yes? The caged birds? Then bring me my jacket. Oh, and make sure the pockets are full of rice. Discreetly, mind. Discreetly full of rice. Rice and cash—feathers and sweets, if you can find any. But *be*

84

discreet.' It was as if he did not want smuggled rice to spoil the hang of his clothes.

The people of Yangcun were told that the courier, 'Sun Swallow', could not be trusted to carry their gifts up to Heaven; the ancestors might quarrel over the gifts or tear him limb from limb. The *birds* would carry them instead; 'Sun Swallow' was an ambassador, and ambassadors cannot operate with their mouths full of tea, and their drawers full of flowers.

So, the gifts were transferred to the birds—tea to doves, locks of hair to finches, questions to linnets, coins (discreetly) to the pocket of the bird-catcher, spices to the side of his jaw.

Then the medium, 'Tongue of Fire', summoned the people to stand behind her in reverent silence, while The Great Miao accompanied 'Sun Swallow' to the brink of the hill, gave him his instructions—and threw him off the edge of the world on a scarlet-and-gold paper glider.

It was a horrible flight. The rice and sweets Miao Jié had pushed inside Haoyou's clothes at the last moment moved about like live insects, up and down his trouser legs, around his ribcage, bunching up in his cuffs and groin, leaking away through the tears in his red silk. He felt like a salt-cellar being shaken empty of salt, a scarecrow losing its stuffing to a gale-force wind. Involuntarily he rained down rice on to the watching host. When his shirt came untucked, he voided feathers like an owl regurgitating a pellet. The coins caught the sun as they fell. The feathers floated down and away, far beyond the town, to be lost on the surface of the river or snagged in trees and spiders' webs. From such a height, there was a danger the coins would gouge holes in upturned faces, or damage tiled roofs. But presently, Haoyou stopped caring.

Nausea enveloped him like a great green towel. His stomach turned to rock, then made a bid to turn him inside out. Fortunately the noise from the bamboo whistles masked the noise of him heaving up his heart.

Down on the ground the people of Yangcun felt the rattle of rice on their heads. It blipped and stung, but it fell like the blessing thrown at a bride and groom—a blessing from ancestors well pleased with the presents the birds had brought them. They saw money embed itself in the riverside mud and sink out of sight. An omen of prosperity, if ever they saw one: the river would surely bring them prosperity now! They found sweets in their bushes and among the chickens. Someone swore he saw a necklace of pearls fall into the river. Someone else said, when she found eggs under her chickens, that they had fallen undamaged out of Heaven.

The mood in Yangcun was transformed. The crowd began shouting up at the kite (though it stood maybe 800 feet above them, small as a red moth). They followed its progress, herding this way and that in order to stay underneath it. The roustabouts reeling it in found themselves engulfed by a huge noisy crowd all shouting out to the kite-rider, all laying hands on the rope.

'They'll drag him out of the sky!' said Mipeng, and covered her eyes with both hands.

The Great Miao caught hold of her wrist. 'Don't. You've seen the future, remember. Nothing takes you unawares.' He was reminding her of her role.

So Mipeng pulled herself up to her full height and commanded the crowds to let go the rope. ' ''Sun Swallow'' will descend when the ancestors have done with him,' she cried.

Hands relinquished the rope, the roustabouts elbowed a space for themselves, and rescued the kite from total destruction by crashing it into a springy green tree. Haoyou was brought down by the bird-catcher with his ladder, and Mipeng began to translate the words of the ancestors:

'Wives, be faithful to your husbands.

'The children born this summer will bring great pride to their fathers, great love to their mothers.

'Send more birds with tea; we have not tasted tea for so long!'

She answered as many of the written questions as she had been able to read as she attached them to the caged birds:

'Do not marry old to young.

'Let the boy try for the civil service: at worst he can fail and at best he may succeed.

'The shop will prosper if you do not overcharge.

'Do not borrow money—the interest rate is too high . . .'

Her audience listened with trance-like attention, drinking in every word.

As the elephants of the Jade Circus rose to their feet, the hawsers tightened, and the boats moved out into mid-stream, Miao Jié paid Haoyou his share of the takings.

It was more money than his father Pei had earned for an entire voyage.

'But it was a trick! We tricked them!' said Haoyou, who had grown older and less innocent since the day before.

'Are we not in the business of tricks?' asked Miao Jié, his dark, narrow eyebrows lifted up in elegant surprise. 'Which is better: to breathe fire and walk a tightrope, or to fetch down blessings and raise hopes? They both make people happy. And that is the object, surely?'

'Nothing I told them was a lie,' added Mipeng. Already her elbows had returned to her sides; her gestures were small, her face tilted down in humility. 'Tongue of Fire' had been laid aside, along with the scarlet robe.

Haoyou looked between them, then at the money in his hands. He could see there was some truth in what Mipeng said. And he could tell Miao Jié was no liar either. The circus *had* made people happy—not least him.

For there is no denying the happiness that comes wrapped up in a fistful of money.

10

The Paddy

The wind died. Summer was coming. Some days drove a wedge of heat between sky and earth which allowed nothing to move—not the trees, not the rice fields, not the river ripples. The only time the wind blew was to herald the sudden torrential cloudburst which daily replenished the water lying in the paddy fields. The Great Miao did not complain. He did not withhold rations from Haoyou and Mipeng because they did not perform. It did not seem to trouble him that Haoyou might not fly again for several months.

'So long as you can fly at Dadu,' he said. 'For the Khan.'

But Haoyou feared the worst. The change in the weather had been so sudden. What if the spirits were disgusted with what he had done at Yangcun? What if, like fishermen round a pool, they had reeled in their fishing lines and were no longer prepared to hook the red kite high into the sky? What if they would never again allow Haoyou to go there and feel the sickening, scalding ecstasy of flight? The worst fear of all, he did not put into words, even inside his own head: that when the wind blew again, he would have lost his nerve.

Miao Jié found them plenty of jobs to do—mending banners, feeding the animals, throwing their messes over the sides of the boats, scrubbing clean the decks. One morning, Miao told Mipeng to help the bird-catcher trap more birds—some to sell in the pretty little cages that the bird-catcher's wife made, some to free in a grand gesture of clemency at the end of each show.

'You're not to go anywhere with that barbarian,' said Haoyou, when she told him.

'Oh no? And are you my husband, little boy, to tell me where I can and cannot go?' said Mipeng, with surprising heat. 'Bukhur has six children, and not one of them older than ten. He needs all the help he can get.'

'He's a Mongol. What would Great-Uncle Bo say?'

'Ah. *That* cultured gentleman,' said Mipeng, and went to learn the art of capturing linnets and orioles.

'They drink blood, you know!' he called after her. *'And they don't believe in baths!'* But she did not seem to hear.

The boats clicked and creaked in the heat. The river moiled and seethed, a dark mustard yellow. For as far as he could see, flooded paddy fields took on a dimpled green sheen as young rice shoots broke the water's surface. Fat black flies converged like pilgrim worshippers on the horses and elephants. One of the Mongol women was calling a name, over and over again, in her high, shrill, ugly tongue: *'Khutulun! Khutulun!'*

Haoyou jabbed the ball of mud he had scooped from the riverbank that morning: it was nearly dry. Poking into it all the quarter-tael coins he had among his savings, he wrapped the clod in cloth and sewed up the edges of the cloth. Then he copied on to it the address of Great-Uncle Bo's house, which Mipeng had sketched for him on the bulwark. There was a boat moored just downstream, bound down river for Dagu. Its owner had said he would deliver a letter to Haoyou's mother. Haoyou examined the odd packet. It was a small fortune to entrust to a stranger, but no one would ever suppose the thing contained money. He had to admit, it was not exactly a letter: Mipeng had not taught him enough yet for him to be able to recount his news. But there was no denying how happy Qing'an would be to receive it. It would rescue her from Auntie Mo's looks of pitying scorn, and from Bo's grudging and condescending charity. It would show Uncle Bo that Haoyou was capable of providing for his mother.

Once again, Haoyou indulged his favourite fantasy: that one day he would be richer than Uncle Bo—richer than the whole Gou family put together—if he ever flew again, that is.

Suddenly, a cool, refreshing breeze, like a spilled tumbler of water, poured along the river. The boats banged against the shore, the paddy crazed into ripples. The river slopped in and out of rat holes in the bank.

It seemed to stir the Mongols from their yurts, for as Haoyou came back from delivering his 'letter', he saw dozens of them out-of-doors, circling their tents, lifting up the heavy, skin panels to look at the yellowing grass underneath, shouting into the dark mouths of neighbouring tents, fetching more Mongols out into the sunlight. Children were running along the little mud walls which trapped the water knee-deep in the endless paddy fields. What were they up to, these restless, never-sit-still ruffians with their saddlebag cheeks and puffy, slit-shut eyes? They were banding together now, closing in on the boat, calling out for the Miao.

'What is it? What's the matter?' called Miao Jié from the boat in front. Whatever it was, the answer made him pull on his boots and run ashore across a narrow, bouncing gangplank. The fresh new wind carried his words back as far as Haoyou. 'Everyone! Everyone turn to and look!'

Everybody was anxious, fretting. The acrobats piled themselves up into a pyramid, the topmost gazing this way and that. Miao Jié sent a small boy up on to the back of the tallest elephant. The lad was on tiptoe, bare feet straddling the protruding spine, hands shielding his eyes. But whatever he was trying to make out, he plainly did not see.

'What is it? What's happened?' asked Haoyou of the juggler, who spoke his own language.

'One of the bird-catcher's children is missing. The smallest one. Wandered off. Disappeared. Probably asleep somewhere under a bush.'

The wind itself joined in the search, now and then sucking the air through its teeth in an anxious hiss.

Everyone seemed to be saying the same thing. 'Probably asleep under a coat.' 'Probably asleep under a tarpaulin.' 'Probably asleep . . . ' And yet their eyes peered downriver, scoured the waterline, searched the flooded landscape for a small figure toddling unsteadily along the fragile dykes of the paddies. Such a deadly playground for a two year old. Such difficult terrain to search.

A rider galloped into the nearest village to ask for help, but the locals were suspicious and chary. They only said that they did not want their paddy walls broken down by ponies and elephants and trampling feet. He rode on to the Buddhist monastery behind the village—a huge building surrounded by a high stone wall. But the saffron-robed monks only looked sympathy out of their famished faces, spoke of the will of God and offered to pray for the child.

Another hour passed, and still she was not found. Haoyou thought of the Gou family searching for Mipeng's sad, mad, missing husband, asking her, *Where will he be? What has become of him?* Like them, he wanted her to be full of magic knowledge. Mipeng might *say* she was not a medium but she *had* found her husband's body, hadn't she? Perhaps if she tried, she could find the missing girl!

But Mipeng was not there. She was out with the missing girl's father, catching birds, both of them unaware of the crisis. Why must she be gone so long, just when she was needed?

'The woman's got six children, hasn't she?' said Haoyou out loud to himself. 'Surely she can spare one?

92

Only a barbarian, after all.' It was what Uncle Bo would have said.

But, inside his head, he kept seeing his little sister Wawa floating face-down in the muddy water of a paddy field, his mother roaming the dykes distractedly, calling, *Wawa, where are you? Wawa! Come here this instant!*

'Khutulun! Khutulun!' Still the mother shouted.

His hand covered Little Dog Wu, faded and prickly. His face turned up to the sky. With his other hand he fingered the bronze collar tight across his Adam's apple. 'Take no notice, gods! A puppy dog is missing, that's all. But we'll find it. Take no notice!' Anything to dissuade the gods from stealing a woman's child away.

The bird-catcher and Mipeng came back just then. Festooned with cages, they stood and listened to the news that little Khutulun was missing, mislaid, probably asleep somewhere. All the captured birds, one moment as shrill as fifes and whistles, suddenly fell silent, beaks ajar, jiggled ever so slightly by the trembling hands of Bukhur the bird-catcher.

Haoyou found himself thinking, *If those birds were just free, they could fly up high up, see everything . . .*

He could not make the Mongols understand him at first; they were too preoccupied to pay him any attention. 'Stupid barbarians!' he shouted at them, and went and asked the Chinese to help him instead: the dwarf and the juggler and the dancer with the wand and ribbon. They slid the big red kite overboard on to the mudflat, and it slumped down between boat and shore, bowing alarmingly.

'There's not enough wind!' said Miao Jié, when he saw what Haoyou was doing.

'There's not enough wind!' said the dwarf.

But Haoyou knew that if the daylight faded, if night came down before the child was found, she would not be found at all. Not alive, anyway.

'There's no high ground!' the roustabouts said.

'You could use my stilts?' the stiltwalker offered, knowing the offer was futile.

'How about the tightrope tower?'

'Or the mast of the boat?'

But the scarlet kite looked more unwieldy with every suggestion.

'The monastery,' said Haoyou. 'And I need the riders.'

The monastery stood oddly aloof from the village, its priests surviving on gifts of rice from the farmers, paying for the food with prayers. They asked if the boy in the red and gold tunic was planning some bloody religious ritual—a suicide, perhaps; they could not condone that, they said. But once convinced that Haoyou was not intending to kill himself, they allowed him to enter.

He was able to climb easily to the top of the perimeter wall from inside, but the kite had to be hauled up the outside, on cords shot aloft by Mongol archers. Banging and scraping the stonework, it looked like a great sleepy moth fumbling its way towards hibernation.

The cords swagged downwards—not to the Chinese roustabouts who usually tugged Sun Swallow aloft, but to the Mongol trick riders. They were seated on little ponies mired to the withers in mud after searching the paddies for half a day.

What a time it took! Every tedious minute reproached Haoyou for thinking up this doomed, time-wasting plan, for occupying people who would have been of more use combing the paddy fields. The child's mother, big-bellied with her latest child, groaned and swayed, holding her sides, clutching the two year old's sleeping shawl, weeping.

The kite reached the top of the wall. Bukhur and Miao Jié tied him to it, buffeted by a fickle, breathy wind already spiteful with droplets of rain. Out of the corner of his eye, Haoyou could see a row of prayer wheels restlessly turning.

He slipped one hand out of its tether to touch Little Dog Wu, and the riders, mistaking it for their signal, dug in their heels and drove the ponies into a gallop from a standing start. The cords went tight, the kite was ripped out of Miao's steadying grasp, and out into empty space off the vertical wall.

The speed flattened Haoyou against the kite as if a giant's hands were pressing against his sternum. For a while he could not draw breath or lift his eyelids. When he did, he thought that the monastery must have crumbled and fallen flat, its grey stone was so far below and behind him. Instead of gliding levelly, the kite was far too vertical. It stalled and began to slump back down, tail-first. Only by throwing his head and shoulders forwards did he manage to level off.

Haoyou peered around him for any sign of Khutulun. Perhaps he was flying in the wrong direction: the child might be behind him: he could only fly *into* the wind, after all. Or perhaps she was inside one of the houses? Or camouflaged with mud? Perhaps she had been washed away by the river long since, or had fallen down between boat and bank. Or perhaps demons had stolen her away.

But at least he could see! He had gained the vantage point of a hawk, the world spread like a table for him to pick and choose from.

The paddy lay like a chessboard, the village a cluster of captured pawns, the monastery the box in which the pieces were kept. Little boats descended the river with barely a wake, whereas those going upstream cut white chevron-shaped scars in its surface. The Jade Circus encampment was no more than a messy scuffing away of the river bank. Water buffalo were all that disturbed the silver sheen of the flooded fields, though here and there a broken mud wall allowed water to trickle from one level to a lower one, making crescent ripples. The very few wading peasants out among their crops were nothing more than discs of yellow in their conical sun hats.

Fear dragged on his stomach like a great sea anchor pulling him back to earth. No! It was not fear, but the tow rope. Looking down, he saw that the ponies had galloped into deep water and were bogged down, unable to move. The tow rope had gone slack, hanging down, adding its weight to the weight of the kite, pulling it out of the sky. There was not enough wind to carry both kite and rope. He slipped the shackle, and the tow rope fell away, a drowning man letting go the lifeline, a dog slipping its lead.

His kite stood alone in the sky.

At once it steadied. Now it was bound to crash, but if he was really lucky, it would descend like a paper dart, smoothly, glidingly, and land somewhere soft and muddy.

And there she was! There was Khutulun! She was floundering up to her chest in the very next paddy. With her head below the level of the mud walls, no one on the ground could possibly have spotted her. But Haoyou could even see the course her little legs had taken her, where the mud levees had given way under her and dumped her into the greening wilderness of water. He could see Khutulun!

When the shadow of the kite passed over her, bamboo wailers howling, she looked up and plainly thought she was seeing a dragon or a demon stooping to snatch her, because she gave a shriek and tried to flounder away, lost her footing and fell face-down into the water. Already exhausted, she barely tried to lift her head clear. Her arms and legs splayed outwards, mirroring Haoyou's own reflection which overlaid it.

'There!' he shouted. 'She's there!' But the only people who could hear him were the Mongols. Would they understand, barbarians that they were? By the time the kite glided to rest, he would be on the far side of the paddy: it might take him ten minutes to wade back to the baby and pull her face out of the water.

Haoyou pushed his feet forwards, threw his head back, raised the kite to the vertical: stalled it in mid-air.

The fabric to right and left of him rattled like a drumskin. Bamboo canes burst through the paper like a skeleton bursting free of its containing flesh. The horsehair tail rushed up between his legs and flicked him in the face. Then he was falling, like a swan shot down by hunters. Hand and foot loops came away from the fabric. Somewhere a bamboo snapped with a noise like a firework. Then the kite flipped over on to its back and plunged him headfirst towards the water, looping at the last moment and landing him on his face not ten metres from the child.

The blow knocked all the air out of him. He could not have drawn breath even if he had not been face down in thickly dirty water. He fumbled with the belt buckle which secured him to the kite, but there was no freeing it. He did not drop his feet, because he thought there would be nothing under him. But then he found both hands clutching young uprooted rice plants, and his knee touched bottom.

The wet kite seemed to weigh as much as the roof of a house—past lifting, it pinned him under water. When he finally pushed his head up into the air, the sun shining through the thick paper of the kite made a red world full of his own bellowing. And as the kite soaked up the water, it grew heavier and heavier and heavier.

When at last he got the belt undone, Haoyou had to squirm out from under, like a mole out of a flooded burrow. He thought an hour must have passed, that he had failed Khutulun for want of the strength to unfasten a belt buckle. His hands were all slime. He had to raise Khutulun clear of the water like a whale scooping a seal out of the surf, and if the Mongol riders had not been there, staring at him from the levee, standing in their stirrups, screaming at him in their impossible language, he did not think he could have found the strength to lunge, slither, stumble, stagger, and crawl as far as the wall of mud.

Only as they slid from their ponies and reached out to him did Haoyou discover that he had no hand to offer them. One arm was full of child. The other hung down to a preposterous length—a monkey's arm; the ledge of his shoulder had quite disappeared.

What did it matter? thought Haoyou. As one of the Mongols threw him face-down over his pony's flanks, he could see his scarlet-and-gold kite—his masterpiece—slowly sinking beneath the muddy water, its bamboos sprung, its skin turned to a bloody pulp. Never again would he fly into the kingdom of the birds, never again prey like a hawk on the spread table of the world.

That's a relief, thought Haoyou, as a blackness deeper than mud welled up and swallowed him.

11

A Patch of Dark

Bukhur the bird-catcher, when his youngest daughter was delivered safe into his arms, released all the birds he and Mipeng had captured that day. He ran from cage to cage, the little girl bouncing on his shoulder, and dragged out fistfuls of feathery panic, throwing them into the air with great whoops of joy and gasping little giggles. Khutulun herself whimpered and reached out mud-caked arms towards her mother, but not until Bukhur had emptied every birdcage in gratitude to the gods, was he prepared to give her over to her mother's scolding kisses.

The Great Miao, after years of working with acrobats and tumblers, was well equipped to put back Haoyou's dislocated shoulder into its socket, and when Haoyou came to, he thought he must have dreamed that his arms were two different lengths. Only one souvenir remained of his plunge into the paddy field. There was a patch of mud which, even when he rubbed his eye, did not wipe away. Plainly a morsel of paddy mud had oozed inside his head and lodged in his brain. Somehow, though, Haoyou could not find it in him to care. He was unaccountably weary, and was developing a headache worse than anything he ever remembered. It never lifted. The only escape from it was to sleep. And while Bukhur and his wife toasted his bravery in koumiss, Haoyou saw it only like reflections at the bottom of a deep well, the sound muffled and echoing, he a distant observer—a kite flyer cruising far overhead . . .

And now he was in the prow of the boat, in the Miao's wicker sleeping shelter. He knew it by the beehive lattice walls which broke the sun into a mosaic on the deck and by the smell of cinnamon. He had a nightmare in which a blue-shirted Mongol came and leaned over him, a bloody knife in one hand, a cup of milk in the other, flicking blood into Haoyou's face. When he woke screaming, only the Miao was there. The Miao seemed to be standing there, whenever he stirred . . . except that he had no head, no hands, no legs . . .

Haoyou slept again, hoping to make better sense of it all when he woke.

At the end of his bed, the Miao's jacket hung on a bamboo cross-tree, like a flaccid white kite. It drifted in and out of focus. How could a jacket stay so immaculately white, amid the filth of a travelling circus? Haoyou wondered, sleepily. And yet the jacket was like the man. The Great Miao was at the heart of the Jade Circus but aloof from it, a strange pristine figure who, even without his red gloves, seemed never quite to touch the world he had created.

Haoyou could see him now—not a dream this time—sitting cross-legged in the doorway of the shelter, silhouetted against the light, long fine hair hanging in an unplaited tail halfway down his back. He was working out his accounts on an abacus. It was that quiet rhythmic clicking which had finally woken Haoyou from his age-long sleep. It came to Haoyou with a rush of embarrassment that he had been sleeping in The Great Miao's own bed, though he did not rightly know for how long.

The boat was moving. Water bubbled soothingly past the hull. The diluted smell of elephant drifted back along the tow rope.

'Dadu soon,' said Miao without looking round. Was

he clairvoyant, too, then? Like Mipeng. Ah, but then Mipeng said . . . Thinking was still painful.

Haoyou rolled his head to the other side and saw a picture hanging from the roof by a cord. It swung with the motion of the boat, making it turn now and then to face Haoyou. It was of a lily, painted in watercolours, every sepal, every petal, every filament of its bare roots perfectly depicted. Haoyou could almost have reached out and plucked the flower off its background. If he had liked lilies. Of course, if Haoyou were ever to own a picture, he would have a boat or a tiger—maybe even a dragon or a horse. But The Great Miao, he supposed, *would* own a picture of a lily, white and fragrant and slightly feminine.

'My father painted it,' said Miao, again without seeming to look round from his accounts. 'My father was a *yinshi*. Do you know what a *yinshi* is, Sun Swallow?'

'I . . . er . . .'

'Never mind.' The abacus clicked like a baby's rattle. 'It is a kind of recluse; one who withdraws from what angers him, rather than show his anger. You are supposed to ask why the roots are bare.'

'Why are the roots bare?' asked Haoyou, wondering what kind of a fool would even notice, let alone ask.

'Because their earth was stolen away.' Miao looked round now, his black eyes alarmingly intense. Haoyou crumpled his face into what he intended for a smile.

'Is it a joke?' he asked politely.

Miao returned a wry smile, but did not say, one way or the other. Instead, he glanced over the boat's side and observed, 'Your friends are coming aboard.' He uncurled his long legs, stood up and reached inside for his jacket, making way for the bird-catcher and two of the Mongol riders who jumped aboard the moving boat. The smell of cinnamon at once gave way to a smell of horses and sweat.

101

In the leather waistcoats which they never took off, the three Tartars almost filled the little wicker cabin. Their leathery faces were obliged to bend close over Haoyou, and when they spoke to him in their impossible, glottal language, their breath stank of koumiss and goat's meat. One of them was holding a bowl of milk into which he dipped his fingers before flicking the liquid wildly over Haoyou, the bed, and most of the wall. A drop fell on the picture of the lily.

'They have come every day since your fall,' said the Miao from outside. 'They made a sacrifice of two sheep, and every day they offer up prayers and a libation of mare's milk to their ancestors for your safe recovery.' Haoyou was too astounded to speak. He stared into the moving grinning mouths of the Tartars reciting prayers of thanks.

'Bukhur's new child is born—a boy. He has named the baby after you. He says he has lost children before, to hardship and sickness. He knows the grief that you saved him and his wife by finding little Khutulun. The Tartars, you see, prize girl-children more than some Chinese. Perhaps that is because they allow women to play a greater part in life.'

Bukhur pulled a crumple of blue cloth out from under his waistcoat and thrust it at Haoyou with a shy smile which showed his ruination of black teeth. Miao translated: 'His wife has made you a shirt. Blue is their colour of good luck. They think it will keep you safer when you fly.'

For the first time, Haoyou remembered his smashed kite sinking out of sight into the mud of the paddy field. Inwardly he made his own prayer of thanksgiving, to his own ancestors, that he would never have to find out whether red or blue was the luckier colour. There again, what would become of him now that he was of no use to the Jade Circus, now that he was no longer Sun Swallow?

Bukhur was pulling gently at his wrist. He wanted Haoyou to go outside with him—to meet the new baby perhaps, or to visit Khutulun and her mother. Haoyou stood up, startled at how unfamiliar his legs felt, how formidably bright the light shone beyond the doorway.

The bird-catcher shouted ashore to the nomadic straggling horde of people and animals walking along the bank, keeping pace with the slow-moving boat. They shouted back in delight at the sight of Haoyou and cast their eyes astern to where, secured to the mast like a sail, hung a new kite even more magnificent than the last.

'They worked on it day and night,' said the Miao. 'They wanted to make it blue, for luck, but Mipeng explained it would never show up against the sky. From now on we shall have to call you Feng—Phoenix, risen from the ashes.'

Tears sprang to Haoyou's eyes: tears of gratitude and terror, tears of affection and of desperation. Now he would have to stay on and fly until he was killed. And yet where else would he have wished himself than among people like this, who thought he was brave and reckless and clever, lucky, unique and heroic, who called him Phoenix and named him in their prayers?

Dadu, imperial city of the deposed Emperors of Cathay, did not begin of a sudden. Its suburbs straggled downstream for miles, squalid and busy and haphazard. Gradually, the houses became more and more densely packed, until it was difficult for the elephants even to pick their way along the bank. The flies which swarmed around the Tartar flocks and horses were no longer horse-flies but bluebottles off the rubbish heaps of Dadu. The smell was no longer of farms and flowers, but of sewage and baking, cooking oil, dogs, smithies, and distilling. Dadu teemed with Chinese citizens and Mongol tribesmen—made Dagu and Yangcun look like villages.

Indeed, the palace Kublai Khan was building was itself as large as Haoyou's home town, to judge, at least, by the vast open space cleared for its construction. Not one tree had been left standing. Heat and light rebounded off its shadeless wasteland like spray off a roof, and the air was full of masonry dust and the noise of rip saws.

The Miao was oddly agitated, his movements quick and lunging, his bearing very upright but with elbows drawn up and fists clasped, as though his hands were wrestling one another. Haoyou assumed it was because the summer had reached Dadu ahead of them: the air was stagnant and still. There might be no wind for kite flying here.

But as the Miao went about organizing a traditional circus performance on the flat site the Khan had so obligingly cleared for them, he seemed to give it only half his attention, his thoughts drifting all the time to some greater worry. He sent the Tartar riders in every direction, giving them instructions in their own language.

A crowd was drawn like iron filings to a lodestone, a crowd larger than any they had drawn on their whole river journey. But the Miao did not even attempt a headcount or guess what their takings would be. When the overseer of buildings came to protest at the circus setting up on the Khan's private property, the Miao did not trouble to argue, but bribed him to go away, with ill-disguised contempt. 'The Mighty Khan would thank you more for telling him of our arrival than for trying to hinder us,' he said, with icy hauteur.

'The Mighty Khan isn't here,' said the overseer. 'The Khan is gone.'

It was the first time Haoyou had seen the circus master lose his composure. A spot of red appeared on his high cheekbones. 'Gone? Gone where?'

'Left for his summer city—for Xanadu,' said the overseer, and took as much pleasure in the disappointment he had given as the bribe he had just pocketed.

The Jade Circus did well in Dadu. Tartar tastes had influenced attitudes in the old imperial city. Chinese and Mongols alike arrived in hundreds to see the acrobats somersault, the singers perform, the riders lean from their saddles at full gallop to pick up gold-painted quinces off the ground, the jugglers balance tent poles on their foreheads, the elephants blow fanfares. These entertainers were no beggar urchins or vagrants tossing oranges in the air, hoping for the price of a supper. Here was glamour and spectacle. When blue-veiled Mongol women wearing silver swords at their hips held out their little shantung collecting bags, no one thought to turn away without paying a few coins for their afternoon's excitement.

Haoyou saw the money. He saw it shared out between the performers. Always Bukhur the bird-collector pressed a few of the coins he was paid into the hand of Haoyou, who had found his daughter. Always there was food and drink for Haoyou and Mipeng. Still Bukhur's wife prayed for Haoyou's safety in the air—even though Haoyou did not fly. Not Haoyou, nor Sun Swallow, nor Phoenix. Even on the days when a wind blew. Haoyou did not offer to fly, and the Miao did not press him.

So no longer could Haoyou lie in his bed, head pillowed on his takings and contemplate what riches he was earning and what he would buy with his great wealth. It was almost enough to persuade him he *wanted* to fly again, actually *wanted* to . . . The beautiful gilt-painted kite hung against the mast gathering city dust: the red badge of manhood he did not dare to wear. Bukhur and the others looked expectantly towards it whenever they caught his eye: they were like children who have given their mother a present and can't wait to see her use it. But Haoyou only averted his eyes . . . and the Miao did not insist. Even when a brisk summer breeze blew up the river valley from the direction of home, Haoyou shook his head and said it would not do. And the Miao did not contradict him.

'It's as if he doesn't care if I fly or not!' said Haoyou peevishly one day.

Mipeng gave a little gusty laugh of annoyance. 'You are priceless, cousin. You lose your courage and the Miao is too kind to make you fly without it. And what thanks does he get? "It's as if he doesn't care"!'

Haoyou recoiled in shock. His right hand, folding across his body, grasped his hurt shoulder. There was no point in arguing. Mipeng had seen through him. Was his cowardice written so plainly on his forehead? Or did she, after all, have magic powers to read the thoughts in his head. After a long and awkward silence, he said, 'I expect you'd like to go home, wouldn't you?'

'*No!*' It was the kind of noise a dog might make if it were stepped on. Haoyou wondered whatever he had said.

In the end, it was the citizens of Dadu who decided matters. Somehow they seemed to have found out about the Jade Circus's flying boy. One afternoon, voices in the crowd began to call out between acts: 'Where is Qiqi? Where is the kite-boy?'

Qiqi? He had not been called that since a hundred miles downriver!

The Miao cracked his white whip and scowled, but the crowds would not be deterred. '*Where is Qiqi? We want Qiqi!*' As they stood on tiptoe to shout, or stamped their feet in emphasis, Haoyou could almost hear the coins jingling in their pockets, the money that would be his on the day he overcame his shameful fright.

As if she sensed his yearning, Mipeng bent to whisper in his ear. She moved Haoyou's hand away from his mended shoulder and over to Little Dog Wu. 'Tell him, cousin. Tell the Miao you are ready,' she said.

Haoyou ran out into the hot, empty flatness in which the circus master stood. 'I *will* fly. I will!'

But Miao Jié frowned down at him as if he was not sure whether he could spare the time. 'There is really no need, boy.'

Haoyou could hear that money jingling now, could remember the admiration of those upturned faces, the great gleaming new kite. 'I *want* to!' he said.

And so he flew. The Jade Circus adjourned to the river, and to the brisk river breeze, to the boats and the great red rhombus of bamboo and silk which hung from the mast. The river wind took him aloft; hot thermals of air over the flattened building site lifted him, in nauseating surges, up and up above the great city of Dadu.

He had never realized a city could be so big! The Tartars had followed Mipeng's instructions to the letter and the new kite resembled the old one, except that the silk fabric was lighter—far lighter and more buoyant. Down below him, the people gave a single gasp, and the noise was like the thermals: it lifted Haoyou's heart so high.

Soon he would be rich—richer than that man down there riding in a rickshaw—richer than that woman being carried in a sedan. He would be richer than Great-Uncle Bo, richer than the apothecary in Dagu who sold powdered tiger bone and sharks' teeth. He would be rich enough to have a dozen pictures hanging on his walls, and not boring lilies either, but elephants and cheetahs! He might buy the warehouse where Uncle Bo worked—buy the ship which had carried Di Chou out of harm's way. He would earn more money than his father Gou Pei had ever dreamed of earning!

And with that, a brightness flashed in the corner of Haoyou's left eye, a flickering shape like a figure running towards him, like a figure cut out of sunlight, fashioned out of lightning. It was so bright it made Haoyou snatch his head aside. The sun breaking through a cloud . . . except that there was no cloud, and the sun was not to his left. Summer lightning, then? Some piece of metal or patch of water reflecting the sunlight back up at him like a catapult?

Haoyou looked to his left and the sky was empty of running men. And yet when he blinked, there it was again—a banner of brightness flapping in the corner of his eye.

'*Father?*'

Why here? Why not at Dagu or along the river at Tong Xian or Xianghe or Yangcun? Perhaps the spirits, like mortals, hanker to see the wide world. Perhaps Gou Pei's ghost had come to visit the Imperial City, to gaze with a tourist's eye at its splendours. And to see his son fly.

'*Father!*'

But the running figure, if it was anywhere, was behind Haoyou now, screened from sight by the panels of the kite. What is more, the roustabouts were reeling him in, fetching him down out of the vaulted sky. He could no longer see any edge to the sprawling city beneath him. Its busy streets, its noise, its soiled air were rising up to meet him.

There were the Tartars, on their ponies, standing in their stirrups to cheer him, and Bukhur festooned in bird cages, his daughter astride his shoulders, awaiting Haoyou's safe return. A surge of affection enfolded Haoyou, as warm as the thermals rising off the bare ground. So what if they did not wash, and what if they did drop their trousers in public? Worse things happen at sea, as his father would have said.

108

There were the elephants, trunks upraised, tasting the dirty yellow air. He realized now how fond he had become of the great lumbering monsters. There were the upturned roof ends to fend off demons descending out of the sky . . . As if they could keep out Qiqi or Sun Swallow or the Phoenix! There were the same marvelling faces that he had seen along the river, and in all his best dreams: people with their heads thrown back and their mouths ajar, loosing all their bodies' ill humours and breathing in the sunlight. Many had waded into the river to get a better view.

And there, plain as day, was the reason they had called for 'Qiqi.' Seated on hired chairs (while all around them the crowd were on their feet), looking like a fat frog and a spindly locust, Great-Uncle Bo and Great-Auntie Mo sat and watched Haoyou drop out of the sky and into the grasp of Mongol outriders who carried him triumphant through the clamouring crowd.

12
Duty

A familiar face in an unfamiliar town is always a happy sight. Haoyou could not wait to disentangle himself from the kite's harness and worm his way through the applauding crowds to greet the head of his family. Was his mother with them? And Wawa? To think they should have seen him perform here, in the Imperial City!

At another level, Haoyou was eaten up with worry. For Great-Uncle Bo had found out—whether now or back in Dagu—that Haoyou was living and working with Mongols—Tartars—barbarians—a race Bo hated above any species of living things. Perhaps he had come to take Haoyou away, to upbraid him with betraying his country, the standards his family had always taught him. Bo probably thought he had abandoned all personal hygiene, never washed any more and did his business in public.

In his headlong dash, he passed Mipeng dressed in her scarlet costume. 'Uncle Bo! Auntie Mo, too! Here!' he panted.

'I know,' said Mipeng scowling ferociously. 'Bo has left the warehouse. He says he chose to leave, but it's my guess he was sacked. He's been pilfering for years.'

'*Mipeng!*' It was an outrageous thing to say about an older relation.

'So he's come where the money is,' said Mipeng, unabashed. The Tartar women with their little shantung collecting bags were passing through the crowd. Haoyou

110

was reminded of the riches to come now that he had regained his nerve.

Those crowds were beginning to disperse, turning for home, still talking about the spectacle of the giant kite. Mothers were saying to their children, ' . . . and don't you ever let me see you trying . . . ' Little children mistook the evening starlings for more kites, more Qiqis. Soon the only figures remaining on the trampled quagmire of the river bank were Bo and Mo, still seated on their hired chairs, hands on knees, graciously ready to accept the kowtow of their niece and great-nephew.

Mipeng had somehow melted away and made herself invisible.

'I am glad you have profited from the opening I found you with this circus fellow,' said Bo, picking food scraps out of his moustache.

Haoyou rushed to tell his news: 'I had a fall—lost the kite—but he put my shoulder back, and Bukhur and Chiggis and Nug and the rest, they built me a new one, and I thought I couldn't—not here, not in the summer, 'cos the wind's not the same inland as it was back home, but then today—well, you saw! It was all right. I mean it was better . . . Is Mother with you? I saw—I saw—I nearly forgot, what with seeing you, and all the cheering. Up there, I think I saw . . . '

'P-lease,' said Auntie Mo, pinching her forehead into thin vertical wrinkles to indicate he was giving her a headache. 'Silence, p-lease.'

The Great Miao approached along an oblique line, setting down his feet with such cat-like softness that his shoes made no squelch in the trampled ground. 'Why, it is the honoured Gou Bo, is it not?'

This time, Uncle Bo did not stand up. 'Is that the day's takings?' he asked, as The Miao passed a crammed purse of money to Haoyou.

'They are his share of the day's earnings, yes.'

'Very good. Then *I* shall take charge of them.'

Bo held out his hands: a greedy little Buddha reaching out for enlightenment. As he reached, the Miao took one step back, so that Bo almost overbalanced out of his chair. 'As head of the household, I must be chancellor of the family's exchequer. How else can Haoyou serve the needs of the Gou clan?'

Haoyou's mouth fell open. Glancing across at the purse in Miao's hand, he found he could not look away from it: *his* proceeds, *his* takings.

'Well?' said Bo with studied pomposity. 'I am waiting, circus master. Your agreement was with me, not with my nephew. I trust you have not been paying *him* rather than me. If so, I shall expect you to give over to me, Haoyou, anything you have earned. You are far too young to have the handling of money.'

Haoyou breathed in, and the saliva in his mouth caught in his throat and set him coughing.

The Miao regarded Uncle Bo as coolly as he might a wayside beggar. Then he handed the purse to Haoyou. 'It is not for me to decide such matters. If Sun Swallow decides to give you his earnings, that is a matter between him and you . . . But just at present, I must ask you to excuse him. The work of a circus does not come to an end with the applause. There are animals to feed, equipment to dismantle. So—sir, madam—your patience, if you please.' And closing his hand over Haoyou's shoulder in a vice-like grip, he steered the boy away, at speed, from the two chairs on the worn turf of Dadu's riverfront.

'Don't give it to him,' said Mipeng. 'You don't have to give it to him. He isn't your father.'

'But he's like my father now,' Haoyou insisted. 'He's head of the family. And he is looking after Mother!'

They crouched together in their sleeping shelter aboard the circus boat, knees round their ears, the disputed money wrapped in a headscarf between them. 'He's a gambler. I told you. He'll gamble it all away.'

Haoyou had never heard this outrageous slander before. Pompous, preaching, yes. But a gambler? Surely not.

'That's why he pilfered from the warehouse. To feed his gambling,' said Mipeng.

'But he's always sitting down!' Haoyou protested as if sitting were not consistent with thieving and gambling.

Mipeng's mouth set into an obstinate line. Her hands were pinioned behind her knees, and she rocked a little, to and fro. Haoyou felt helpless and bewildered. In all his life no one had ever taught him anything but blind obedience: to his parents, to his elders, to his fate.

'Do as you like. It's your money. But if you want to be rid of it, why don't you just burn it on your father's shrine,' said Mipeng.

Haoyou gave a little cry of recollection. The scene with Uncle Bo had quite put out of his head what he had seen—up there in the sky, out of the corner of his eye.

'I saw him!'

'Saw who?'

'Father!' exclaimed Haoyou. 'I saw his spirit— somebody's spirit. This last flight. Don't look at me like that: I did! I saw a spirit. It must've been him!' He tried to conjure up the picture in his head, but the flicker was elusive, masked out now by the irritating, ever-present patch of paddy mud which had lodged in the side of his eye.

Mipeng looked doubtful. 'Maybe he came to warn you Uncle Bo was coming . . . Don't rub your eye like that: it can't be good for it.'

113

He knew she did not believe him about the spirit, but what could he do? He could not take her up there and show her, could not take anyone into the sky with him. It was his preserve and his alone. What happened up there was between him and the Dead.

'If he's there next time, I'll know,' he thought aloud to himself. 'I'll know he wants me to obey Uncle Bo.' It was like throwing a coin up in the air to decide a question: heads or tails. Except that he was the coin.

'Why shouldn't it mean he wants you to spit in Bo's eye?' asked Mipeng. But he chose to ignore her.

Uncle Bo and Auntie Mo had to be shown hospitality. They had travelled a long way: the first time either of them had left Dagu. An hour or so later, they presented themselves at the side of the boats, looking peeved and insulted, clearly expecting to be taken aboard. Peeping through the lattice of his sleeping shelter, Haoyou could see them shifting from foot to foot, coughing and humphing, waiting for their great-nephew to appear and offer them accommodation. But there was no room on the boats.

'I can't leave them standing there,' he whispered guiltily. 'I'll give them money to find a room in Dadu.'

'Let them find their own room,' said Mipeng. 'They chose to come, didn't they?' Her rudeness shocked and unnerved Haoyou. He physically shrank away from her. Then he heard Miao Jié up on deck, explaining about the lack of space.

'We can share with the boy,' said Bo. 'My wife and I have suffered enough already in travelling here. I suppose we can endure a little more discomfort.'

But just as the Miao was about to lose patience, Bukhur the bird-catcher came rolling up behind the pair, in his bandy, horseman's gait. Auntie Mo gave a great bleat of alarm and dodged behind her husband, who stepped backwards on to her feet as Bukhur began a fulsome speech accompanied by wild hand gestures.

The Miao covered his mouth for a moment to conceal a smile, then said, with utmost gravity, 'Bukhur has heard you are kin to his friend, Sun Swallow. His respect for the boy has led him to pitch a yurt for you and your excellent wife.'

'A what?' Bo shook off his wife, who was still clinging to him.

'A yurt, sir. A tent.' The point of his whip pointed out the dozen Tartar homes, brown and shapeless as molehills, where the hog-maned horses stood about in hobbles, children ran around naked, and dogs barked incessantly. It was hard to tell the difference between the yurts and the elephants who sat nearby, legs folded under them.

'I can't sleep in a stinking pile of goatskin!' cried Bo, jerking his feet clear of the ground in his excitement, while Mo nodded her head in urgent agreement.

Haoyou could not stay hidden and hear such offence given to Bukhur. He poked his head up, trying to look as if he had just woken up. 'You're welcome to sleep in my shelter up here, honoured Great-Uncle. Mipeng and I will sleep in the yurt. If you like?'

Bo looked triumphant, and bellied his way aboard, passing Auntie Mo his shoulder bag to carry. She set it down, signalling for Haoyou to fetch it. But then, catching sight of Bukhur again, still grinning his toothless smile of welcome, she picked up the bag and, clutching it to her chest, picked her way aboard as awkwardly as a three-legged cat negotiating a garden wall.

They must have thought Haoyou's quarters would be luxurious, whereas, in fact, there was barely room for two slight people to crawl under the awning and stretch out. Their two bedrolls took up all of the floor.

'This is contemptible,' rumbled Bo. 'You a kingpin of this circus and you have to sleep in this . . . this . . . *beehive*!'

Mo, meanwhile, mewed peevishly like a seagull, and held the small of her back, anticipating how uncomfortable she would be. 'Fancy him sharing sleeping quarters with the medium,' she muttered, as if Mipeng were not present. 'Most improper. Most.'

'The yurts are very comfortable . . . probably,' said Haoyou, still feverishly trying to please his honoured relations. But Uncle Bo cut him off short. Lying down on his back on the deck, he managed, by grunting and paddling his feet, to slide himself under the awning. His straw slippers remained sticking out. Auntie Mo whimpered at the thought of the space left for her. Then the big bullfrog voice resounded through the frail wicker mesh of the shelter. 'We shall review the situation in the morning.'

Haoyou and Mipeng managed to reach the shore before they were overcome by giggles. They collided with Bukhur, and swept him along with them, the old sheep-skinned nomad looking perplexed but thankfully not offended. 'I feel terrible!' said Haoyou, hilarious and tearful both at once. 'I don't think honoured Great-Uncle realized . . . '

'Never believe it,' said Mipeng. 'He wanted a chance to search your belongings for your money.'

'Mipeng!' Once again, her bitter disrespect shocked him to the core. Then he glanced back over his shoulder, at the boats. 'If you're right, he's got what he came for. I left my money under my clothes.'

'No you didn't,' said Mipeng, and held up her sleeve-ends for him to see where she had hidden the headscarf full of coins.

* * *

The yurt was dark and warm and smelled so powerfully that it was like sleeping in a stable among the animals whose skins had gone into making it. There was an unseasonable fall of rain during the night. It drummed noisily on the yurt and woke Haoyou, but not one drop found its way inside. 'Uncle Bo won't know to go below decks,' he said aloud, assailed again by guilt. 'He doesn't know those shelters leak.'

'By now he does,' said Mipeng's voice out of the darkness.

'Why do you talk about him that way?' asked Haoyou refusing to laugh.

'Because I have no respect for him. Great-Uncle Bo is a mean-minded, greedy, selfish dishonest bombast.' But Haoyou had put his fingers in his ears. He had not *really* wanted to hear her reasons.

Mipeng's disrespect went against everything twelve years of life had drummed into him. Respect is everything. Without Respect, the sun can fall off its hook, the stars run down out of the sky, the earth blow away. Without Respect and Obedience, all doors stand open to Chaos and Disorder. As his fingers loosened in his ears, he heard the word 'bombast'. What was a bombast, he wondered. But, unable to ask, he fell asleep again and dreamt of Uncle Bo squeezed into the bucket of a war catapult, being shot into a sky full of cormorants and exploding like a bomb into a thousand thousand fragments, each one a spinning silver or copper coin.

In the morning, Great-Uncle Bo, glaring at any member of the Jade Circus who passed by, declared that he had never passed such a night and hoped never to pass such another. Auntie Mo looked like the cat which fell in the river but died, not of drowning, but of being wrung dry.

They were both so angry that Haoyou fully expected them to up and leave.

But Bo said only that he was going into Dadu to find a bath house. He stood, then, looking at the sky, going nowhere, coughing from time to time so that his big throat bulged explosively. Haoyou stood by, head bowed respectfully, until Auntie Mo stuck her cold, sharp nose behind his ear and hissed. 'Where are your manners, boy? Where is your etiquette?' Haoyou was expected to advance the cost of the public bath. He did so at once, holding out a palmful of coins for Bo to take what he needed. Bo's long nails scraped the boy's palm as he scooped up all the money.

And when Haoyou went to the deck shelter, he found both bedrolls had been slit down the sides. Their costumes had been turned inside out, Mipeng's collection of bird feathers pulled out of their jar and strewn about. As she gathered them up, she looked at Haoyou as if to say, *What did I tell you?*

'Perhaps he was looking for my manners,' said Haoyou wistfully.

Great-Uncle Bo had not returned from the city before Haoyou embarked on his evening flight. If he had looked down as he rode the hot, dirty wind, he might have seen Bo seated at a table in one of the small residential squares, playing dice with the old men there, his free hand covering a pile of winnings.

But Haoyou was not looking down. He had a rendezvous to keep with the spirit he had glimpsed the day before. His mind was not on the gasps of the crowd, the money in their pouches, the riders galloping to catch him as he descended. He could think only of his father, his funny, wiry, agile father whose hair smelled of sea

118

salt, who could draw a ship with seven strokes of a brush and sing sea shanties that made the baby sleep. Whatever question Haoyou had asked him, Pei had always had an answer—straight away, no stopping to think: why the sea was blue, why fish out of water smell bad, why pandas eat bamboo. His answers might not have been true about the octopus ink, about the bathhouses at the bottom of the sea, about the pandas being Buddhists . . . but Gou Pei had never left a question unanswered, never.

He would tell Haoyou now where his duty lay. Had ownership of Haoyou and his money passed from father to uncle, like a wheelbarrow or a hat? Or was he free to make his own way in the world?

Weather conditions were strange: a thick haze pinned to the ground by a layer of fast-moving wind. From up in the sky, Dadu was barely visible, its buildings no more than a handful of stones at the bottom of murky water. Haoyou felt more detached than ever from the little, ground-bound men and women who could not fly. He forgot the rope tethering him to the ground, forgot the men down there on whom his life depended. All he could think of was finding his father, of meeting the spirits face-to-face.

Nothing. No one.

The money was no longer important. Haoyou would have given every cash of it willingly, just to see his father again. Panic seized him, because when he tried, he could not remember his father's face or voice. With increasing urgency, he combed the landscape of clouds for the real thing—for the brightness of Gou Pei's spirit running towards him across the mare's-tail clouds.

'Father! Father, show yourself! I swear I'll be a good boy! I'll do whatever Great-Uncle tells me! I promise! Only let me see you! Let me!'

The kite handlers were starting to haul him down. The

119

kite gave that familiar flick, jerking his head back on his neck . . .

And there it was. Over to his left, just out of plain sight, a flicker, a flapping, like a sheet caught on a pagoda. A brightness shaped like a man. *'Daddy!'*

Haoyou turned his head so hard that he ricked his neck. He twisted his body so wildly that the kite stalled and dropped, and he had to pitch his shoulders forwards to level off again. The breath sobbed in his throat. The shape flickered in his eye, but would not stand where he could see it, would not look him in the face. His eyes stung and ached with the effort of trying to look sideways; in the end he had to close them. 'Are you well, honoured father?' They were the words he had used every morning since he was big enough to speak them. 'Are you well, honoured father?' He could even smell the tea he had offered each morning, along with the words.

No reply. Nothing.

'Did I do right? Did I? Must I work for Uncle Bo?'

But he knew the answer already, for he had made a bargain with the spirit world. And he knew inwardly that his father would not speak to him until he showed the perfect obedience of a good son.

The riders had no sooner caught hold of the descending kite than Haoyou was struggling free of the harness. He thudded down to the ground amid the horses' hooves: an inelegant landing. He barely noticed the applause of the crowds. Only the long white whip of the circus master flourishing its ribboned tail reminded him that he also owed a duty to the Jade Circus. So he allowed himself to be carried back to the show ground on the saddlebow of Bukhur's eldest son, spreading his arms theatrically, like bird wings. The women went among the crowd in their blue veils, holding out their blue collecting bags, and then the hubbub of Dadu families moved away like ripples from a great splash. They went home talking of the Phoenix and how brave he must be to fly.

As before, Uncle Bo and Auntie Mo were left behind by the departing crowds, like twin daubs of graffiti. One fat circle, one thin line. Mo looked harassed and anxious. Bo had stayed at the gaming tables until his last coin was gone.

The Great Miao knew, at one glance, what Haoyou had decided. He looked oddly upset—even scared—by Haoyou's resolve.

'Well, great-nephew?' boomed Uncle Bo. He had been eating nothing but pickled onions all day, and the words emerged along with a sonorous belch. It made him sound even more like a great bulbous bullfrog. 'Have you decided to obey your head-of-family, or must I beat you again? You will grant, I suppose, that I have the right to beat my own great-nephew?'

The tip of the long white whip came to rest on Bo's corpulent stomach. 'I might have a thing to say about that,' warned The Great Miao.

But Haoyou went and knelt down in front of his aunt, pressing his hands together, bowing his head till his forehead touched her bony knees. Next, he shuffled sideways, guiltily aware of the stains he might make on the newly cleaned scarlet costume, and made obeisance to his great-uncle. The whip tip touched him on the shoulder, reminding him, 'There is no need to do this, Phoenix.'

'Yes there is.' Haoyou reached inside his tunic and pulled out the bank notes he kept hidden in the lining, behind Little Dog Wu. Miao Jié made a noise of exasperation. Mipeng, arriving at the last moment, burst into tears. 'There are coins, too. I'll fetch them later. I've seen my father, you see! Just now! And I promised to be a good obedient son,' said Haoyou, his forehead pressed against Uncle Bo's fleshy knees.

'Fetch the coins,' was all Bo said in reply.

13

About-Face

Having done what he thought was right and honourable, Haoyou was rather taken aback that people were so cross with him afterwards.

Mipeng would not even speak, and went to sleep at the far end of the boat, with only the stars for shelter, sooner than share a roof with him. Even The Great Miao seemed hugely put out. In a great outburst of agitated energy, he wrenched the Jade Circus away from Dadu and sailed on upriver, bypassing whole villages and towns without giving a performance, urging the boys to walk the elephants faster. Bo and Mo sat in rattan chairs at the stern of the lead boat, Mo armed with a fly whisk to knock the flies from her husband's head and shoulders. Now and then she nodded in the noonday heat, then a cry would be heard filtering back along the cluttered decks: 'Fly, wife! Two flies! Wake up!'

Haoyou had hoped, after treating Bo like a father, some sort of love would kindle similar to the kind he had felt for Gou Pei. It did not. Uncle Bo persisted in seeming pompous, surly, and unkind. Haoyou had expected to feel some pang of virtue, but it did not come. He worried in case his father's spirit (willing now to speak to him) would be left behind by the breakneck speed they were making. He was also worried that Uncle Bo would not have had a chance to dispatch money to his mother, and that she would have nothing to live on. Not that he dared to ask directly.

'Was my honoured mother well when you left her?' he asked, as obliquely as he could.

'I left her in good hands,' said Bo. 'She can consider herself a fortunate woman . . . Now, when is this barbarian going to moor up and put on a show? We cannot earn while we don't perform.'

'Miao Jié's not a Mongol, Uncle,' said Haoyou, still nervous of Bo's lifelong hatred for barbarians. 'He's from the south.'

'He who lies down with dogs gets up with *fleas*,' said Bo, emphasizing the last word so heavily that Auntie Mo, roused from a doze, hit him with the fly whisk.

When the river grew too shallow for the boats, they disembarked and continued on by bullock cart. Lush watered grain fields gave way to rocky grassland where the shadows were purple and the earth so light that the wind kicked it up into little scurrying whirls. For a week they travelled.

Summer dust settled on them in such quantities that when they woke in the mornings, it was as if they had slept for a hundred years and been buried under decayed decades. The nights were as cold as midwinter, the moon congealing like ice on a black pond. The days were so hot that the red panda died of dehydration and for want of its natural fodder. Trees had been planted along the road, to provide shade for travellers, but they were not the same trees as grew in Dagu, and the wind blowing off the Steppes had bent them all in one direction, as if they too yearned to go back the other way.

The Chinese, like sailors approaching the edge of a flat world, grew nervous and disinclined to go on. Like bright butterflies they could see no merit in a landscape without flowers. The Mongols, on the other hand, became more and more cheerful. They were heading back beyond the Great Wall, to a land they understood. Its mile after mile of featureless, rolling plain held no terrors for them. Any faces they met from now on would be Mongol faces.

'Where are we going?' wailed Uncle Bo, bewildered by the Miao's failure to mount a single performance. Auntie Mo as a-twitter with anxiety, certain that Mongol bandits, any night now, would kill her in her dust-filled bed.

'Ask him, nephew! Ask him!' Bo demanded. 'We have a right to know where this trek is leading!'

So Haoyou, unwilling but still determined to obey, presented himself at the door of the circus master's tent. He saw that Miao Jié was sitting cross-legged on his sleeping rug, holding the picture of the lily between both hands.

'My honoured uncle respectfully asks . . . where we are going next,' said Haoyou bowing from the waist.

'If he asks it respectfully, it will be the first time in his ill-mannered life,' said the circus master still studying the picture. Then he looked up, and his face was ashen. 'I'm sorry. It is unforgivable to insult a man's kin. I apologize.'

'That's all right. I'm not a man yet, am I?'

The Miao signalled that Haoyou should enter. Since no one ever entered the yurt of the man-in-white, it was like being invited into a lion's den by the lion. Haoyou went in and sat down. There was a noise of precious silk tearing. Haoyou swallowed hard. Another mending task for Mipeng. Because the rip was too loud to go without comment, he said, 'I'm growing again. I'm sorry.'

A chart lay open on the ground. He fixed his eyes on it in the hope of fixing the conversation there too.

'You place great store by the virtue of Obedience, don't you, Sun Swallow?' said Miao.

'Pardon?'

Miao struggled to simplify his language. 'You believe you have to do as you are told, at all costs.'

'I thought . . . I mean, yes. I thought that was my job.'

The Miao tossed his head irritably. Thinking he was still failing to make himself clear. 'I don't mean obeying *me*, boy.'

'No, neither do I. I meant . . . I thought that's what children had to do. My father always said: Boys must obey their parents. Their heads are closer to the ground. They cannot see so far ahead as their elders.'

'Your family are Confucians, I suppose.'

Haoyou was unwilling to comment in case it was the wrong thing to be. 'He got mentioned a lot in our house. Confucius.'

'Mine too. Though my mother was a Nestorian, and me, I lean towards . . . ' The Miao pulled up short of such an intimate confession. ' . . . though I dare say we each follow the gods it suits us to follow. In answer to your uncle's question, this is where we *were* going.' He pointed on the map to a sketchy outcrop of tents and pavilions denoting some kind of settlement. Though Haoyou knew nothing at all about maps, the paper round about Miao's finger looked suspiciously empty of nearby towns. Just mountains and rivers.

'Were?' was all he could think of to say.

'It is Xanadu, Swallow. Summer capital of the Great Khan, pleasure garden of the Conqueror.—Don't rub your eye like that.—But I have changed my mind. Tell me, Haoyou, would you have done *anything* your father commanded you?'

'My father?' It was a relief to be asked such an easy question. Haoyou gave a broad smile. 'Oh yes. Anything. I've always obeyed Papa.'

The Miao's lips drew back from his teeth in an expression which was half agony, half rage. Haoyou's smile froze. 'I was afraid so. For many years I was the same. Many years. My beliefs were at odds with my father's, and yet wilfully to disobey . . . I always knew it would be like crossing into a wilderness. Obedience is the cement which binds a family together. Am I right?' (Haoyou felt safe to nod vigorously; it sounded like something a boy ought to agree with.) 'For the last year— more—nearer two years—I have been on a journey of discovery, Sun Swallow. But your . . . your *good example* has rather shaken my resolve. It reminded me too much of my own childhood: so safe—so bounded by . . . *obedience*. I no longer quite know how my journey would end, if I were to reach Xanadu. SO!'

He suddenly leapt to his feet, like a spring uncoiling. It made Haoyou recoil so fast that there was an even louder tearing of silk. 'So, Swallow! I am turning back. We are turning back!' Even in saying it, the tension went out of the circus master's face and colour returned to his cheeks for the first time since Dadu, along with a broad, boyish smile. 'You may tell your honoured great-uncle that the Jade Circus is no longer bound for Xanadu and the court of the Mighty Khan! As a hater of barbarians, I am sure he will be glad to hear it. Go now. Go! *Go! Go!'*

Haoyou ran from the tent as fast as his legs would carry him. Xanadu? The name was rich with mystery and promise—aswarm, too, with terrifying associations: the lair of Kublai Khan himself. Haoyou did not know whether to be glad or disappointed. Was he not, after all, to perform in front of the Mighty Khan, as the Miao had always promised? Was the Jade Circus really turning homewards—towards Dagu and Haoyou's mother and Wawa and the sea?

Instead of telling Uncle Bo, he went first and told Mipeng. He thought she would be pleased.

'You see what you've done?' she berated him. 'Now he'll never find the answer.'

'What answer?' said Haoyou, bewildered. 'Answer to what?'

Mipeng stamped her foot, ablaze with irritation. '*I* don't know, do I? But he's travelled thousands of miles to meet Kublai Khan, and now, because of you, he won't keep the rendezvous . . . *aiya*!'

Haoyou's shoulders drooped, and he dragged his feet as he went to tell his great-uncle and aunt the good news that they were going home.

But he was kept from ever delivering the message.

As he scuffed his way back towards his tent, dodging between the tumblers and the hoop-throwing juggler, a noise of hooves made him look round.

For all they wore the same mailed fur jackets, the same conical fur hats, Haoyou saw at once that the riders approaching were not part of the Jade Circus. The sun glistened on drawn swords, and they were bearing down on the encampment as if they would kill everyone in it. They slashed through guy ropes, rode over folded yurts and cooking fires and bundles of belongings. They hacked down one of the cart buffalo which fell to its knees with a startled grunt, streaming blood. And they fired arrows into the great scarlet kite where it hung from a pole.

Haoyou rolled between the seated elephants and tried to hide himself between their grey flanks.

The Jade Mongols, who had been drinking the night before, tumbled confusedly out of their yurts, but every one of them was armed, and stood now, sword in hand, shoulders hunched forwards, feet apart, ready for a fight.

The attacking soldiers—there were thirty or forty of them—formed a half-circle around the camp, while a man with a face as weathered as his saddle wove in between the tents surveying everything as if he had just secured it in battle. When Bukhur went out to salute him, birdcage in hand, the horseman rode not *up* to him but *at* him, making him step out of the way two, three, four times over.

Every member of the Jade Circus, Mongol and Chinese alike, looked towards the tent of The Great Miao. When at last he emerged, he was dressed as if for a performance; hair tied back, one red glove in his left hand, the other folded over his belt, the folds of his trousers drooping elegantly over the cuffs of his immaculate boots. The white whip was in his hand. He looked as unassailable as a snowy mountain peak.

On either side of Haoyou, the elephants stirred in the odd silence; he thought he would be crushed between the two bulging grey flanks. The noise of their gurgling digestion deafened him to what the Miao was saying. It was said in the Mongol tongue, anyway.

Lacking a piece of vocabulary, Miao Jié snapped his fingers, without once detaching his eyes from the rider, and the Jade horse-trainer supplied it instantly.

The elephants, to whom Haoyou was a novelty, began exploring him with their trunks. That was when he decided to take his chance in the open. The rest of the Jade Circus began to emerge from hiding. The Miao announced them, one by one:

'*I give you Kung Wa, whose knives fly like the darts of love!*'

'*I give you Huang Yuping who has danced before the thrones of princes!!*'

And, being performers, they rose to his expectations of them, bowing, turning somersaults, or producing a bird from a silk scarf. The juggler threw three of his hoops into the air. The rider watched the hoops rise and drop. So did his horse.

'*And here is Phoenix, the boy who flies! This sight alone is worthy of royal eyes!*' declared the Miao.

Haoyou spread his arms wide, dipped his head, hoping to convey both splendour and respect. There was a long silence during which the cart buffalo fell over on to its side and died.

128

Then the rider wheeled his horse about and galloped out of camp, the rest of his men closing ranks behind him into a tightly packed stampede which raised up the dusty soil like a column of smoke in their wake.

Auntie Mo came moaning and quacking, leaning heavily on Mipeng. 'Circus master! Are we spared? My husband must know! Are they coming back? Will they kill us? Are we going to die?' She was as shrill as a corncrake.

'Indeed no,' said The Great Miao, soft spoken once more. 'On the contrary: we are to follow the way they have gone. Imperial outriders. Royal bodyguards. It seems that an army is travelling east—yonder, beyond that horizon. To think: we might have passed one another and never met. An opportunity lost.' The circus master closed his eyes for a moment, and breathed in through flared nostrils. 'Instead, madam, we are summoned into the imperial presence. Make ready to travel. Tomorrow we perform before the Great Kublai—the Mighty Khan himself!'

14

The Mighty Khan

Apparently, the Khan had been roused from his summer capital at Xanadu by some flurry of rebellion within the vast territory which was now his khanate. With one general poised to invade Japan and another in the deep south, chasing the latest self-styled 'Song Emperor', Kublai had decided to ride out and suppress the unrest himself. He was willing, however, to let the Jade Circus entertain him and his troops now that their ways had crossed. In fact, he was very partial to circuses.

The Great Miao was like a kite string taut to breaking. He had abandoned his pilgrimage of the soul, his two-thousand-mile trek to look the Khan in the face, only to find that the Khan had come to *him*, was within a day's ride. Instead of a ghost haunting the Miao's imagination, the Khan would soon take on flesh and blood, a face, a smell, a tone of voice, a reality. As the circus made its lumbering way in the direction the horsemen had gone, the Miao took a horse and rode a parallel course, but so far off that he was almost out of sight.

Auntie Mo was in a state of nervous collapse. For thirty years she had listened obediently to her husband's lectures on the vileness and barbarity of the Northern invaders. She had not questioned his descriptions of their cruelty, his instructions to pray for the Song dynasty to prevail against these forces of darkness. Now, a thousand miles from home, Bo seemed to have slipped out of his opinions like sand out of a sieve and left her alone, still believing all Mongols were murderers looking for someone Chinese to murder.

'If only we could get home to Dagu,' she said, fifteen times, whispering it in at Mipeng's ear, pleading, wringing the girl's upper arm between her bony hands. The sentence was never finished. A wife who complained that her husband was a drunkard and a gambler was the worst kind of traitress. So Auntie Mo clutched and trembled and nagged Mipeng to look into the future and say how it would all end. And when Mipeng refused, Auntie Mo nipped her with her long fingernails and told her she deserved strangling as a disobedient hussy.

Mipeng hardly seemed to notice. She barely flinched from the pinches and slaps. Her eyes remained fixed on the distant Miao Jié. But when, at one point, his white horse disappeared from sight, she broke free of Mo and begged the boys to let her ride astride one of the elephants—a most unseemly thing to do. When Haoyou, running alongside, asked what she was doing, she said abstractedly that she wanted to keep the circus master in sight.

'Why? Do you think he might run off?' said Haoyou, in a panic. But Mipeng only gave him another of her cool, withering looks.

The camp of Kublai Khan appeared, at first, like a wilderness of mole hills, the yurts of his vast retinue changing the sere, silver countryside to a grey brown. It was not an army but a nomadic tribe on the move, with all its women and children, its grazing stock and horses, its baggage carts, portable kitchens, workshops, shrines, and war machinery, perpetually migrating between nowhere and somewhere else; between boredom and excitement. The noisy wealth of Dadu, the fabled parks and pavilions of Xanadu were of only passing interest to the Mongol mind which was always anxious to be moving on, especially if there was a good fight waiting at the end of the journey.

The Imperial Outriders returned now, surrounding the Jade Circus and herding it onwards, to the heart of the camp, past caged lions, leopards, and lynxes, and aviaries holding hundreds of gerfalcons. As they passed a cart filled with the Khan's possessions, the circus hands caught sight of a huge mechanical tiger, its counterbalanced head rocking in the breeze so that its hinged jaw opened and shut, opened and shut. Then they found themselves standing in front of the pavilion of the Mighty Khan himself.

The Khan's yurt was made from otter and marmot and ermine furs, hung with cloth of beaten gold and panels of painted silk, and the floor was strewn with tiger skins. Porcelain vases of cobalt blue and dazzling white stood on tables of lacquered black-and-gold. A couch of plush magnificence supported a rather portly man with whitish skin, black eyes, and a large, hawkish nose. He was dressed in Chinese robes and was discussing a drawing with a young, Tibetan-looking man seated at his feet.

At the sight of Miao Jié, he beckoned him in, holding out the drawing for him to see. 'What do you think?' he asked, speaking excellent Mandarin Chinese. 'Aniko here is designing me a Buddhist temple for the park in Dadu— according to the principles of *feng shui*, of course. I take the very best advice. What's your opinion?'

'It speaks peace and endurance,' said The Great Miao, from his knees, staring at the design. He had had no time to prostrate himself, before the paper was thrust in front of his face. 'It is . . . lovely.'

'He is designing me another for Xanadu. A goldsmith by trade. Gold and jade. But his gifts are many. What an artist!'

A fine-beaded sweat sprang from Miao Jié's face. He looked up at the Tibetan goldsmith as if he had found a fawn living in a tiger's den. Touching his forehead to the

132

ground, he recovered his feet and returned to the members of his circus, like a man sleep-walking. 'Chinese,' said the Miao. 'Chinese architects. Chinese artists.' And no one could tell from his face whether he found that admirable or shocking.

Everywhere they looked, cattle and horses were grazing, their fat rumps as white as new-sprung mushrooms. They looked liked ghost mares, ghost cows—white and perfect—with never a gall or whip mark. Their milk would never be drunk by any but Kublai Khan and his children.

'Shall we set up?' asked the roustabouts.

The Miao did not answer at once. He looked unnerved, afraid. Haoyou wondered if he might be ill: so pale, so listless, mesmerized. 'It seems . . . ' he began. 'It seems too . . . ' he said.

The roustabouts looked uneasy.

'Expect he's worried the circus isn't good enough.' That was Haoyou's opinion.

'He's worried about the grass being wet.' That was the stilt-walker's idea.

'He didn't expect it to be like this,' said Mipeng.

Haoyou looked impressed. 'Can you read his mind, then?'

Mipeng snapped back at him with unreasonable heat. 'I have eyes, don't I? I can *see* it, can't I?'

But nobody else could make head nor tail of what the Miao was thinking, so mired did he seem to be in his own thoughts.

'I bet he thinks the Khan will cut his head off if the show isn't good enough,' said Haoyou. It came out louder than he meant.

The Great Miao turned and paced out the length of the tightrope, marking the positions for the end towers with a scuff of his foot. It brought him back in among them. His face gave a peculiar twitching grimace which might have been anger. But though he grabbed hold of Haoyou's hair, he did not rend it out. 'In that case,' he said, in a strangely hoarse whisper, 'I . . . if that should arise, Sparrow, be sure to tell him that a *carpet is required*, and not an axe.'

They debated it, Haoyou and Mipeng, as they checked over the kite. The arrow holes left by the Khan's knights had all been mended, but it had not been used for so long that dust from the journey clouded its livid red, and obscured its delicate patterning. The bamboo whistles were clogged with dust and grass.

'What did he mean, "a carpet is required"?'

'Did he ever say anything to you?' she asked. 'After you were hurt? When you were in his shelter?'

'About needing a carpet, you mean?'

Mipeng pulled a face. 'Not exactly.'

'I was asleep all the time.' Haoyou checked the harness to see that its leather had not become dry enough to crack. Haoyou told Mipeng about the picture of the lily, its roots bare, robbed of its soil. He could see that his words meant something to Mipeng if not to him. 'You know what's coming, don't you?' he said, peevish that she knew and was not telling him. 'You've seen into the future, haven't you? You know what's coming. I can tell.'

Once again, she flared up at him. 'Then you don't know much, do you? It's just as well you don't have to earn your living as a clairvoyant!' But he got the impression she was more scared than angry. 'Do you never *sense* that something's wrong, cousin? Am I a medium because I use my eyes? Am I a medium because I notice things? Is that why all mediums are women and not men . . . AND DON'T RUB YOUR EYE LIKE THAT! How many more times?'

Chastened, baffled, Haoyou took his hand away from his eye and put it over Little Dog Wu instead.

'You don't have to do this,' said the circus master as they climbed the dusty slope overlooking Kublai's camp.

'I want to,' said Haoyou, hoping the Miao would not shame him by referring to his temporary loss of courage.

'I can tell the Khan the wind is wrong. You don't have to do this.'

'I want to,' Haoyou insisted, thinking of his father, waiting for him up where the clouds were piled like fleeces on shearing day. 'My great-uncle says he'll flay me if I don't.'

The Miao made a snorting noise. His face was a picture of contempt. 'Is this the same great-uncle who called the Mongols barbarians and demons? Is this the same great-uncle who declined to sleep in a Tartar yurt?'

Haoyou did not want to switch his attention from the ropes and harness to the white, sweat-soaked face of the circus master. Such unexplained torment chipped away at Haoyou's concentration and he needed to concentrate.

'He says the Khan is a fruitful tree where we should take shelter.' Haoyou winced as he said it. He, too, was secretly astounded by Bo's change of heart. What Bo had in fact said, when he saw the Khan's magnificent possessions, was, 'There's a tree worth plucking! You pluck it with both hands, boy!'

'The wind's good here,' said Haoyou.

But The Great Miao hardly seemed to be listening. 'A man shouldn't go against his own conscience,' he said, though he said it as if it were a question.

There was nothing for it; Haoyou would have to tell the truth. 'Look, I have to fly. My father . . . My father's

135

spirit is up there. I've seen him. I want to speak to him. I think he'll speak to me now.'

'Your father?' Disbelief, regret, and pity entered the circus master's face all at once. 'And what would your father say about you flying to entertain the Kublai Khan?'

'I don't know. I'll ask him, shall I?' Haoyou gave an irritable tug at the great long ropes which, by their sheer weight, tethered him to the ground. He did not like being disbelieved.

They laid the kite down on the hillside. 'What if he were to forbid it?' said the Miao, and as he reached across Haoyou to fasten the harness, Haoyou glimpsed the haft of a knife inside the white jacket.

'He'd be a bit late, wouldn't he?'

Three furlongs away, Kublai Khan sat on a gilded wooden throne, his wife beside him, an assortment of children at his feet, a white cheetah tethered by a lead to his chair leg. The wind made the sparse silvery grass lap like water around the rim of the bamboo frame; it was like floating on a raft out at sea. The roustabouts came tramping uphill, ready to raise the kite to the vertical and lift it into the air, but the Miao drove them away with an awkward slash of the white whip. His spittle blew away in the gusty wind as Miao Jié knelt over Haoyou and spoke into his face. His right hand reached inside his jacket to close around the knife. 'I know what *my* father would have said.' The Miao spoke so softly that even the roustabouts would have been unable to hear. 'My father left me in no doubt. He said it every day before his death. He made me swear to it. And since when did a boy defy his father and his family and his fate? Eh? *You* wouldn't. *You* didn't.'

Haoyou was certain now that he had failed in some crucial test, and that the Miao was about to sacrifice him, like a Mongol goat, to the memory of a tyrannical father. He twisted his head as far as possible away from the face above it, though he could not take his eyes off that knife. The knife was half out of its sheath. *'Don't! I didn't know! What did I do?'* he shouted into the white face looming over him. He shouted it so loud that the roustabouts reared up their heads.

The Miao blinked. His face contorted once again with inner agony. He let the knife slide back into its sheath. His hand came down on Haoyou's face and, though Haoyou pulled away, he could not prevent the palm resting down over his eyes.

Then the Miao was brushing the hair back off Haoyou's forehead. 'All my life I tried to be an obedient son. Like you. To do my duty. Like you. Like you did with your absurd uncle.' His voice was gentle again, rich with the music of his southern dialect. 'Why did you have to set me such a good example, Sparrow?'

Understanding sharp as any knife dug Haoyou in the ribs. 'What did your father make you swear, master?' he asked.

The Miao had moved round to the top of the kite, above Haoyou's head, and began heaving the frame up off the ground, lifting the kite into the face of the wind. The strong breeze flattened the silk against Haoyou's body, raised up the hair on his head. But it could not wash away the remembered feeling of that hand resting on his face.

'What did he make you promise to do, master?' said Haoyou again.

From behind him the soft sing-song voice replied: 'To kill the slayer of Emperors, naturally. To kill Kublai Khan.'

15

Miao's Journey

The Jade Circus gave a dazzling display. Beside the opulence of the Royal Family, the bright circus costumes looked all of a sudden tawdry and garish, but there was no denying the talent inside them. The Great Miao had taken care to gather the best, the most novel acts, the best schooled singers and musicians. The jade-green banners were no longer lofty when flying among the massed colours of a conquering army, but the skill of the jugglers was no less, the daring of the acrobats, the spectacle of the whirling ribbons, the glamour of the dancers.

The Mighty Khan watched with benign enjoyment, pointing things out to his children, remarking to his wife. He sent his compliments to the singer and asked to see the knife-thrower's knives, checking the sharpness of the blades with the flat of his thumb, then nodding and grinning and waving the performance on.

The horsemen appeared to bore him, for his own cavalry kept in training with similar riding tricks, and were mounted on better horseflesh. He had seen elephants before in greater number and armed more excitingly with flame-throwers rather than Chinese ballerinas. Flame-throwers were more to his taste. But the conjuror made him stare, and the Szechwan clown made him laugh uproariously by laying a gigantic china egg then hatching it out into a goose.

Then, off the slopes of the nearby hills, there rose a distant butterfly trailing a single thread. The wind was fickle. The butterfly rose haltingly into the air, jerked back several times into the path of the wind, as it threatened to fall back to earth. Finally, catching a thermal of warm air, it climbed into the blue. A row of men, like a tug-of-war team, moved gradually backwards across the landscape, playing the kite, paying out more line, coaxing it higher and higher. And Kublai Khan saw that the kite was manned. A slightly built boy was slung from a harness beneath it, and beneath him were trailers of ribbon, a cascade of horsehair, a twinkling of tiny mirrored sequins catching the sunlight.

The Empress Chabi gave a cry of admiration. The Khan rose to his feet. The Royal Bodyguard laid arrows to their bows as the kite moved overhead. An eerie whistling was the only sound to be heard. The white cheetah, feeling a shadow fall over it, arched its snowy back. Kublai Khan beckoned the circus master to him. The Miao ran to answer the summons, one hand covering his heart in polite obeisance.

Looking down, Haoyou saw Miao run towards the dais, his hand over his knife, and let out a despairing cry. *'Oh, Papa don't let him! Don't let him do it!'* he begged, hanging now directly over the throne. *'Papa, save the Khan!!'*

The Khan, his round face beaming, grabbed hold of the top of Miao's sleeve excitedly. 'Who is he speaking to?'

'To his ancestors, Lord Khan.'

The answer seemed to cause the Khan no difficulty. 'And can he see deer?' Realizing that he could easily ask for himself, he bent back his head and bawled, 'Can you see any deer, boy? Deer? Deer!'

Haoyou looked around. He could see chickens and rabbits, a brace of dead swans swinging at the tail of a kitchen cart. He could see the white mares whose milk no one but the Khan and his family were permitted to drink. He could see the elephants of the Jade Circus drinking from a trough. He could see a postal rider galloping across the land, raising a wake of red dust. But as for deer . . . There was a clump of squat trees growing beside a dried-up river bed where deer might just shelter . . . But he could see no deer.

As he looked desperately round, though, twisting his eyes into the very corners of their sockets, he did spot the familiar bright figure running out of the sun, making him point and shout: *'There! There, look! There's my . . . '*

Away went Kublai, calling for his hunting elephants, loosing his cheetah, mustering a ragged band of ministers, officers, and noblemen for a hunting foray. He went in the direction Haoyou had pointed, jabbering excitedly about the novelty of having a huntsman in the sky.

The kite settled to the ground amid bemused performers whose audience had suddenly jumped up and ridden away. Unapplauded, undismissed, the members of the Jade Circus stood alert and unmoving, all facing the way the hunt had gone. They stood so still that they might have been the hollow terracotta figures who stand guard over the royal dead.

Twenty minutes later, the Mighty Khan and his huntsmen came galloping back. Haoyou closed his eyes, imagining the anger of a barbarian warlord sent on a fruitless excursion by a worthless flying boy.

But no! There, dragging behind one of the horses, bouncing slackly over the thin grass, slid a big fallow deer roped by its feet. Haoyou gave thanks. He understood now, why his father had darted out of his hiding place in Heaven. He had come in answer to Haoyou's prayer, and flushed that deer out into the open.

Chance, coincidence, never entered his head . . .

Equally relieved, The Great Miao gave the signal for Bukhur to release his caged birds, signifying that the performance had come to an end. Kublai nodded delightedly and sent for gold to reward them all. His huntsmen, meanwhile, released their peregrines and hawks, and watched delightedly as their hunting birds plucked every last songbird out of the sky and delivered it back to earth mangled and bloody and dead.

'My name is not Miao,' said Miao Jié, sitting cross-legged on the floor of his tent. 'Where I come from, in the south, it is the most common name. I chose it so as to . . . sink myself in among the working people, out of sight.'

Haoyou had no idea why the circus master should choose him to confide in—even less why he should allow Mipeng—a mere woman—to hear the secrets of his past. They had only come to get paid, and here they were, sitting on the Miao's square of carpet, drinking his tea. Haoyou kept wanting to ask, 'Should I send my cousin away?' But Miao Jié, having once begun talking, allowed no space for interruptions.

'My ancestors are of good family—noble blood—a family on which the Song Emperors have always . . . relied: advisors, ministers, tutors to the young heirs, husbands for their daughters. Confucians, of course. My father was a man of absolute integrity, totally devoted to the Imperial Family. Each in turn, the sons of our family have devoted themselves totally to the welfare of the Royal Household, and to preserving them in time of danger. Naturally, when the Invaders came, my father pitted himself against them. We all did. But I was only a child, the youngest of seven brothers. When my brothers put on armour, I was left behind to complete my studies. So I saw things as if from a great distance, you understand? I saw Kublai cross the Great Wall like the sea washing over a row of pebbles. We began with all the advantages: strategy, new weapons, knowledge of the land . . . and yet

141

the Mongols kept coming, sweeping us aside, absorbing it all, turning every advantage against us until we were being killed by our own cunning.

'I was left very much in the charge of my mother's Nestorian priests: fools most of them—muddled thinkers— riddled with superstition. But there were things they said that . . . rang true. I found myself thinking the unthinkable—that my father's way was not the only way.

'And then there was so much death—so much slaughter! The old Emperor died. His heir was a sickly boy. Soon he was dead, too. If the gods meant the Song Dynasty to rule, surely they would have spared a Song prince to do it! But no. The stock was barren. Just to find a new Emperor it was necessary to look further and further afield—for a "true heir"—huh! Father even crossed into Kampuchea, looking for a Song heir . . . '

The circus master took a long shuddering breath. 'I believe the war is lost,' he said, looking straight ahead, his eyes resting on the wall of the tent but not focused, not seeing. 'I believe there is only one battle left to win. And that is to come to terms with losing. To accept. To draw a line. To submit to Fate. That's a kind of obedience, too, isn't it?' (It was an appeal, the way Miao said it.) 'Otherwise what? People like my father—people like me— we are just rocks in a river bed. Obstinate obstructions, waiting until the river pounds us into grit. I want to do better than that! I want to think like History. I want to look Kublai Khan in the eye and understand why the gods have entrusted Cathay into his hands! *That's* a kind of obedience, isn't it? To God? To the will of God? To the will of History?

'I've tried hate. I've tried jealousy, believe me! My father would have spent me and my brothers like seven coins to buy back China. But where's the end in that? China could beggar itself, spending its sons on perpetual war. There must come a moment when we say, "Stop. Enough." Of course my opinions made me a traitor in the eyes of my father. I was a traitor to think it. I betray my ancestors by thinking it.' His face was stony white. The picture of the lily, held in the angle of one knee, twisted out of shape as he rocked to and fro.

'But you're not! Anyone can tell that!'

Haoyou shot his cousin such a horrified look that she ducked her head and her short hair swung forward and covered her face.

'But you swore all the same,' said Haoyou, fixing his eyes on the spot where he knew the Miao carried his knife. 'You swore to ki—'

'*Shshsh!*' said Mipeng. It was such a sudden noise that Haoyou jumped and spilled his tea. 'His father was riding off to war, wasn't he? There was a chance Miao Jié would never see him again! What else could he do? Break his own father's heart?'

Miao inclined his head, acknowledging the truth of what Mipeng had said. 'After he . . . Later, I decided to make a journey—however long it took. No matter how it ended.'

'To find out what the Khan was really like!' said Haoyou.

But Mipeng contradicted him. 'No. To look his demons in the eye,' she whispered, and the Miao stared at her like a man who finds his pockets have been picked without him knowing.

'Oh, don't mind her,' said Haoyou apologetically. 'She reads minds.' He did not really understand, but at least the Miao's chief ambition did not seem to be assassination. Still . . . he thought he had better make sure. 'You won't . . . er, um . . . you won't try it, will you? Because then he'd probably boil us all in oil. The whole Jade Circus. Probably.'

Miao smiled patiently. 'Yes. I think he would, Sparrow. I think he very probably would. Rest assured, I shall bear that in mind.'

'And anyway—you don't hate him, do you? Yourself, I mean. Do you? Not like Uncle Bo did, or your father. I mean, you're like me. You don't mind them. You don't see any difference between them and us. They're just good riders to you—or bird-catchers or whatever.'

The Miao winced. 'That's not entirely true, Sky Sparrow. Not entirely.' Inside his head, The Great Miao, second cousin to the Emperor, travelled again through his childhood, a place normally confined to bad dreams. 'All of my brothers died fighting at the battle of Qinxa Jiang. My three sisters did not reach Kampuchea alive: the journey was too hard for them. My father was captured. He had royal blood in his veins. The Khan is sensitive . . . ' Miao Jié broke off with a kind of a bark. 'The Khan has always shown scrupulous *respect* for royal blood. He does not believe it should ever be spilled on the ground . . . '

An aching kind of hope arose in Haoyou, who understood all about losing a father. Perhaps somewhere the Miao's father was still alive, painting his flower pictures, cursing the Khan under his elderly breath.

'So he did not behead my father,' the Miao went on. 'Instead he—'

'STOP!'

This time Mipeng made them both jump. Haoyou gasped at her temerity. She had actually leaned forward and *put her hand over the royal mouth*! And yet the circus master did not appear to mind. He covered her hand with his own, and let her speak. 'Stop,' said Mipeng again, in a gentle whisper. 'He's only a boy. His head is already hung with too many bad pictures. No more.'

As they walked back to their own tent, Haoyou told

his cousin off roundly for interrupting. 'I wanted to know what happened to his father!' he complained.

But Mipeng changed the subject. 'Tell me, cousin: what would you do if First Mate Di Chou had come to your house at New Year and killed every one there. Everyone. And all the chickens, too?'

'I'd hit him and punch him and kill him and pound him and stab him and stamp on him and rip off his . . . '

Mipeng laid a restraining hand on her cousin who was jerking himself off his feet as he wrestled an invisible enemy. 'Quite,' she said softly. 'So please remember: that is how Miao Jié feels inside. It is not very easy for a man to push the plug back into a volcano like that.'

Haoyou hung back, scuffing his feet, letting her go ahead. 'It's not fair,' he carped. 'It's easy for you. We can't all look inside other people's heads, you know!'

Haoyou's head was so full of images and speculation that he was looking forward to his bed. He would lie in the dark, turning them over and over, like the day's booty. He was working for a member of the Imperial Song family! A man of royal blood! He had performed for the Mighty Khan, Conqueror of all Cathay, and the Khan had *spoken to him*! 'Can you see any deer, boy?' He had given Haoyou gold—Tibetan coins sent in tribute from the Roof of the World! Miao Jié had looked into the eyes of Kublai Khan and not felt obliged to assassinate him. And though the Mongol army might press on tomorrow in one direction and the Jade Circus in another, all in all it had been an extraordinary kind of a day.

'*Psst! Nephew!*'

Haoyou struggled back from the brink of sleep to find his great-uncle kneeling over him. '*Where's the money?*'

'What money?'

145

'The gold the Khan gave you!'

'But—I was going to send it to my mother and Wawa!'

'Nonsense. I can put it to good use. I've made this wager . . . ' He took hold of Haoyou's hair and coaxed him out of the tent by it.

Encouraged by Miao Jié's earlier talk of defiance, Haoyou dared to persist: 'I want to send it home to Mother. It's special. From Tibet! I want her to see it!'

'Gold's gold,' said Bo, clearing phlegm from his sinuses. 'The Khan's men are waiting for me. Now do as you are told.' He had been drinking koumiss: Haoyou recognized the smell on his breath. Times had indeed changed if Great-Uncle Bo, head of the Gou family, was drinking fermented mare's milk with Kublai Khan's Mongol warriors.

Haoyou tried again to insist, but being half asleep, he did not phrase it as well as Miao might have done. *'It's for Mama! You can't wager it! You always lose!'*

Bo took hold of Haoyou's collar in one fist and tried to lift him off the ground. The collar tore. 'Don't tell me what I can and cannot do with my own money, cub! I have to invest! On behalf of the family, I have to exploit the stupidity of these oafs while we have the chance!'

'The Khan's knights, you mean?'

Haoyou could see Trouble stampeding towards him like a herd of Mongol horses.

'All drunk as fishes, of course,' said Uncle Bo, swaying like a tree in a gale. 'Saw my chance while their wits were awash. They were bragging about those birds of theirs.'

'Birds?' Sweat sprang through Haoyou's palms. What had his uncle wagered? That Haoyou could outfly a falcon? Climb higher than a hunting hawk?

'There were a couple of their birds overhead, scrapping like starlings. Feathers raining down. "Seen better fights between chickens," I told them!' (Haoyou was amazed that his uncle had said it and been allowed to live.) 'Then I told them about fighting-kites—the ones you built back in Dagu—the sport of it—the excitement.'

Haoyou gave a gasp of laughter. The relief! 'Yes! Yes! I'll build them fighting kites, I can do that! I never built any in Dagu, but I could, yes! I'll do it tomorrow! They will, they'll like that! If they like their hawks fighting each other, they'll love fighting-kites!'

But Haoyou had been over-quick to rejoice. The drunken bragging had progressed from hawk-fighting to fighting-kites, from fighting-kites to man-carriers. Bo had boasted of the uniqueness of Haoyou's act, and the knights had pooh-poohed the danger. Then had come the inevitable challenge: '20 taels say you can't do it yourself!' (Uncle Bo had made several such bets in the past and won every time: drunken braggarts always backed down in the daylight.)

But the Khan's knights had not only taken up Bo's bet, they had upped the stakes to 100 taels, saying, 'The first man down is the loser'.

'They'll never do it,' said Bo confidently smacking his lips at the prospect of his biggest-ever win. 'Or else they'll kill themselves trying. They don't even have a kite, huh!'

The torn collar of Haoyou's shirt hung down, revealing the rim of Haoyou's hidden purse. With more speed than Haoyou would have credited, Bo snatched the Tibetan gold pieces, and bumbled back towards the roasting-ox revolving over a blazing, hissing fire. Haoyou could see his big grinning face squeezing itself in between the grease-smeared beards of the Khan's knights, affirming the wager, depositing the stake money.

The bet was clearly on.

16
Fall From Grace

The Khan's retinue included every kind of craftsman. There was nothing which could not be achieved if a knight of the Khan wanted it. So, by morning, to Bo's sorrow, there were two kites in the camp, two man-carriers, the second styled exactly on the scarlet wind-tester. It was blue, of course, to bring Mongol luck, but it was in every other way identical, even down to the Chinese characters scrawled on the panels. After all, the Mongols were always adapting Chinese inventions; if Chinese magic symbols enabled a Chinese boy to fly, then the Mongols, too, would use them.

The challenge was set for just before dawn, when the wind first rose and there would be no one around to intervene. Bo had kept Haoyou with him all night, making him sleep (or rather lie awake) between Auntie and Uncle, a cord threaded through his metal collar and tied to Bo's wrist. Such was Bo's trust in his great-nephew's obedience.

He was right to doubt it. Left free, Haoyou would certainly have gone in search of Mipeng—where was she, anyway?—knowing that she would go straight to the Miao, knowing that the Miao in turn would forbid it. Unable to move—scarcely able to breathe—Haoyou had to content himself with praying inwardly to his father's spirit. 'O honoured father! Honoured Gou Pei! Please help us to win the money! Great-Uncle needs it for Mama and Wawa! We need it to send home! Don't let the Tartars run off with the stake money, Papa! And please, Papa! Don't let Uncle make any more bets after this!'

Finally he dozed off, only to be woken minutes later by Bo tugging on his hair. Morning was pale beyond the open tent flap. They went in search of the roustabouts and, by promising them a cut of the winnings, Bo secured both their help and their silence. The giant red kite was taken down soundlessly from its cross-tree, and joined the blue one on the hill nearby. Like mirror images, the kites confronted each other: a red butterfly admiring its reflection in a blue pool.

Although Bo had thought one of the *knights* meant to undertake the challenge, they had no such folly in mind. Instead, they had found themselves a belligerent, shaven-headed Mongol youth called Chiggis, with ears like stirrup leathers and a neck like a raw meat-bone, and told him he had to do it. He was not much older or heavier than Haoyou: the kite would easily lift him. The only thing which might undo him (Bo observed hopefully) was the armoury of weapons he wore at his waist—a hatchet, a dagger, a cattle goad, and a slingshot. Haoyou found very little comfort in looking at them.

The two teams of rope-men eyed each other with surly antagonism. The Khan's men had bribed some member of the Jade Circus to show them the knack of launching a man-carrier, and though the culprit was not actually there, helping them with their rope, his handiwork was plain to see. Whatever they did not know, the Mongols watched, then copied slavishly.

Haoyou rose into the gloom, closely followed by Chiggis: two damsel flies hatching within the same minute. The sky was still freckled with stars. A sinking sickle moon looked like one of those blades tied to the strings of fighting kites.

No sooner was Chiggis off the ground than he gave a shriek of terror and began cycling furiously with his feet, flailing his arms, begging his rope-team to set him down

149

again. Haoyou smiled grimly to himself. This was going to be easy. The blue kite staggered and crashed back to earth. Chiggis landed amid curses and abuse, like a pigeon falling into a thorn bush. Bo hurried over to claim his winnings.

But the knights greeted him with drawn swords, saying there had been no launch. They had been practising, they said. They had still to launch their man into the air. Meanwhile, they threatened little Chiggis with fists and daggers, until he was more afraid of them than of the kite, and agreed to go aloft again.

This time, he shut his eyes and screwed his leathery face into a grimace so horrible that it looked like a fresh cow pat. His shrill shriek continued steady, on one pitch, a lesser man's lungs would have been empty of air. It only stopped when the rope team jerked the kite so hard that they winded Chiggis. Before he could recover his breath, he was ten fathoms into the air and it was too late to change his mind.

Glowering at the unsporting knights of the Khan, Bo retreated, trying both to express his disgust and avoid turning his back on their sword points. 'Just take him high and keep him steady,' he told Haoyou's rope team. 'All we have to do is keep him high and steady and wait for their man to crash.'

The rope team neither needed nor wanted his advice. Now that they stood there, lined up parallel to their Mongol rivals, they were quite eager enough to give of their best. This was Chinese against Mongol, Cathay against Tartary, and for one brief moment, on this brightening hill, in the middle of nowhere, the battle odds were even again.

Haoyou, too, thought that all he had to do was go high and keep steady. He prepared himself for the cold, the nausea, the shocks to his spine when the rope jerked. But the Mongols had not taken on the bet with a patient wait in mind.

By the time Chiggis reached the top of the sky, he had achieved the same frame of mind as a warrior going into battle: a pitch of hysteria which blinded him to the possibility of death. He gurned at Haoyou. He pulled out the slingshot and a pebble from his pocket. On his back-swing, the kite gave a terrifying lurch which the rope-team countered with a sharp tug. It shook the grimace off Chiggis's face. His hands and feet flew out in all directions. The slingshot struck the frame with a resounding crack and bounced back to hit Chiggis on the head. The pebble dropped out of its pouch and plummeted to the ground, harmless as a bird dropping. Haoyou could not help laughing out loud.

Chiggis gave a roar and tugged the hatchet out of his belt. The Mongol rope team set off at a run, dragging their man closer to his opponent.

'You fools! If the lines tangle—!' Bo blustered, but he was invisible now, irrelevant to either side in this War of the Kites.

'You fool! If the lines tangle . . . ' shouted Haoyou into the wind. But there was a kind of joy in the extra pang of fear which came when he realized Chiggis was trying to kill him. Haoyou was in his element, after all. He wore his kite like a magician wears his cloak. As the blue kite closed on him, he had only to tilt the plane of the red one to skirt away downwind, side-slip with all the grace of a fish eluding a crab.

Down on the ground, the Mongol team lumbered towards the Chinese one, looking to barge them off their feet, but the Chinese were too quick for them, running with their rope caught under their armpits, taunting the Mongols with laughter.

Hatchet raised, Chiggis swept wildly past, roaring like

a heifer. But he could only shake his hatchet like a baby wagging its rattle. Haoyou stuck out his tongue.

The Mongols, enraged beyond endurance by their Chinese counterparts, let go the rope of the blue kite, and a full-blown fight broke out, men wrestling and punching and rolling on the ground, while the rope ends slithered unattended, away through the grass, like confederate serpents. The sun's disc, topping the horizon, lifted both fliers higher by its warmth, and the rope ends were lifted clear of the ground and out of reach—bell pulls hanging from the clappers of twin bells, red and blue.

'Demons! Barbarians! Fools! Idiots!' Bo's great figure bounced down the hill like a flaccid goatskin bottle, as he ran for help to break up the brawl. The Miao came from his tent, black hair streaming as he ran, his feet bare. The Royal Bodyguard slashed through the hobbles of their horses and leapt into their saddles.

Chiggis saw what had happened to the ropes, and the hatchet dropped from a hand too slippery with sweat to hold it. Haoyou, appraising the situation, balanced his body carefully, carefully and watched his long morning shadow crossing the ground. If the trailing rope end touched ground someone might still grab it and get back control of the red kite. If it tangled in a tree, the kite would drop out of the sky like a broken parasol. His only hope was to hold scrupulously flat and level—a red saucer floating on a choppy sea. Chiggis had no such knowledge to comfort him. He bawled and shook his fist at the men on the ground who had forgotten him, cast him adrift in a strange ocean. The blue kite tilted and side-slipped—almost crashing into the red one just below it. Murderous to the last, Chiggis drew his knife and slashed at Haoyou as their faces rushed together. The blade struck the red silken fabric and there was a noise like a drumskin splitting. But the wildness of the stroke unbalanced the blue kite.

Chiggis's face emptied of all its grimacing fury; the mouth shrank to a small black O, the eyes widened. Then he dropped—a riffling, rattling, blue bundle of spills and cloth and boy and harness and rope and screaming. Forty fathoms below, a tree—the only tree for miles around— exploded, scattering a miasma of shimmering green leaves, as Chiggis lost his battle with gravity.

Miao had almost reached the trailing end of Haoyou's kite-rope when he tripped and went head-over-heels. From nowhere, Mipeng, wearing a white jacket (but with her legs shamefully bare), was joined by the Szechwan clown, the stiltwalker, and Bukhur's second son in a wild and headlong chase to catch hold of the rope and save Haoyou from crashing. It eluded them, like wool teasing a litter of kittens.

Chiggis's crash put a sudden end to the brawl on the ground. The Mongols staggered to their feet, gaping and cursing, and looked to the knights who had employed them, fearful of punishment.

Bo, one sandal lost, crouched like a question-mark, feet splayed, gulping air and grinning like a wolf. The 200 tael were his! He had won!

But the knights of Khan did not lose a bet so easily. Ignoring the fact that their kite pilot hung dead from the branches of a tree, they took out their short Tartar bows, and each laid an arrow to his bowstring. 'Our man not down on ground!' they called out to Bo and, narrowing their eyes against the dawn brightness, began to set about shooting down the red kite.

Never had Haoyou known such terror. Nowhere to take cover, no means of running! He was a sitting target—a great clumsy red bird offering its soft underbelly to a volley of unstoppable arrows. It took them three shots wide of the mark before the knights began to find their distance.

'Stop!' shouted the circus master. 'I forbid it!'

'Stop! Please!' shouted Mipeng.

But the knights only laughed, showing two or three yellow teeth at the back of empty gums.

Bo, seeing his winnings about to disappear in front of his eyes, waddled gasping as far as the tree, his one sandalled foot slapping the grass. He began reaching up on tip-toe, trying to catch hold of the wreckage of the blue kite, to pull it out of the tree. Chiggis must touch the ground before Haoyou!

Meanwhile, an arrow ploughed between Haoyou's spread fingers and through the red silk, as cleanly as a hot needle. The fabric stripped the fletches clean off the arrow, and they alone remained embedded in the small round hole. He side-slipped, losing height dangerously fast, moving away from the hill and out over the Khan's camp, now alive with running figures. Another arrow struck the frame of the kite and glanced off it.

Bo had managed to get hold of the wrecked kite's rope, but it was tangled round a branch, and though he tugged with all his might, the tree only bobbed and curtsied, lending the appearance of life to the dead, dangling Chiggis.

Haoyou managed to detach the rope from his harness and drop it to earth. He was coming down much too fast, and there would be no one to catch him out of the air. He needed somewhere to land—somewhere soft. A yurt perhaps? But the tent poles of a yurt might impale him. An arrow struck him in the sole of his shoe and stuck there, the point like a fire lit in the arch of his foot. He saw Kublai Khan himself emerge from the royal yurt, his skin jacket ablaze with golden scales of armour plate.

And there it was! A cart full of soft earth and dry grass! Haoyou even had time to wonder why anyone would bother to transport a cartful of earth and dry grass. Collapsing his shoulders, he lifted his arms up high above his head. 'Skin-a-rabbit!' his mother had always said, as she pulled off his shirt at bedtime . . . He brought forward his knees, and the red kite stalled. From a height of twenty feet, he dropped into the cart as sweetly as a bale of hay into a haywain. Canes snapped, silk tore, Little Dog Wu shut his eyes, and the soft loamy red soil exploded around Haoyou like flour off a baker's table.

'Don't get down! DO NOT GET DOWN, you worthless son of a wet worm! STAY IN THE CART!'

From on top of the cart, Haoyou could see his great-uncle shouting, but the distance between them was far too great for the sound to travel. He supposed he had won the bet—Great-Uncle Bo would be well pleased with him. But at what a cost! He only hoped Chiggis's family would not blame his death on Haoyou. Without a doubt, the circus master would be angry . . . but even that could not dim the sheer joy of being alive. His father's spirit had delivered him safely back to earth! He knew now how a dancing crane feels which runs the gauntlet of hunters' arrows to land safely on its nest. It was with a grateful heart that Haoyou pulled the pierced sandal from his foot and jumped down from the cart.

'Your man first down, *tajik*!' triumphed the knights of the Khan, spitting at Bo as they swaggered past him. They did not even trouble to recover Chiggis from the tree: he was no one of any account.

Miao, white with rage, cracked his white whip above Bo's head as he passed, and said, *'Go back where you came from, Gou Bo!'*

Kublai Khan, like everyone else disturbed by the morning's excitements, looked in the direction of the great red awning slumped half on and half off the ornate cart of earth and grass, and the boy standing alongside it on one foot. 'Fetch that *defiler* before my face!' said the Mighty Khan, Ruler of all Asia and Cathay. 'He has desecrated the holy places and offended the spirits of my ancestors. Why is his head not rolling on the ground? *Let me see him dead!*'

17

Loyalty and Betrayal

The soft earth on which Haoyou had landed had been shovelled up one thousand miles away, the grass reaped and dried on the Steppes of Central Asia: earth and grass from the birthplace of Kublai Khan. He prayed to his ancestors in front of it; he poured on to it libations of koumiss and blood. Haoyou had landed on the travelling altar of Kublai Khan, and if he had landed on the Empress Chabi herself, he could not have committed a worse offence.

Within seconds, he had been forced into a kneeling crouch, his arms twisted behind his back, forehead pressed to the ground, neck bared for beheading. Soon he would need no kite to fly around the hollow vaults of the sky, being no more than a voiceless, headless flicker of light.

'The fault was mine!' called the Miao, still breathless from running.

'Why? Did you tell him do it?' asked the Khan, scarlet with anger.

'No! It was his uncle's fault!' Mipeng gestured wildly over her shoulder, although Bo had somehow melted out of sight.

'So! Uncle is fined one nephew. Cut!'

The bodyguard set one foot on Haoyou's back. He rested the blade of his sword on Haoyou's neck to target his stroke.

'He can only go where the spirits send him!'

That was Auntie Mo. Thin and white as a heron, she

stood with one hand clamped to her chest and the other reaching out, as if Haoyou might still be plucked from danger. 'Isn't that right, boy?'

But Haoyou was past speech. He banged his head on the ground. The mud in the corner of his eye shivered and glimmered like burning turf.

Mipeng saw the Khan glance momentarily skywards, and blessed Auntie Mo in her heart. 'It is true! My worthless cousin only flies with the help of the spirits! They draw him up into the sky. They set him down again. I am his medium, Mighty Khan!'

This time the Khan's eyes shot towards the tree crowned with the blue wreckage. The Miao took over the argument: (Kublai Khan would never allow himself to be swayed by a woman). 'This morning he was challenged by your knights. The ancestors of Tartary—up there in the sky—looked on! They chose the winner! They chose whom to set safe down again on the earth. See where they set him! What plainer sign? The boy was fated to please the Mighty Khan, not to anger him!'

The bodyguard spoke no Chinese and could not follow the argument. He raised his sword for the blow. It was the smallest of gestures from Kublai's round brown hand which commanded him to hold off a moment longer.

And it was in that moment that Bukhur the bird-catcher chose to help his friend Haoyou the best he could. He stretched his old bones out on the ground and called, 'Very useful boy, this, Almighty Khan! He is Eyes-in-the-Sky. Deer he sees! Lost children he finds! Why not enemies? Ambushers? From the sky nothing is secret. He can be the Almighty Khan's eyes in the sky!'

Superstition and conquest. Almost by accident, almost without intending it, Haoyou's friends had appealed to the Khan's two strongest compulsions. He signalled that Bukhur should get up and walk aside with him, to explain what he meant. Out of the corner of his good eye, Haoyou could see his old friend the bird-catcher waving his arms, pointing up at the sky, over the horizon, now miming archery, now throwing invisible objects, now mimicking explosions: *'Bchhh! Bchhhh!'*. The bodyguard passed the time flicking Haoyou's hair around with the tip of his sword.

By the time Bukhur and the Khan returned, Haoyou was a member of the Imperial Army—a reconnaissance pilot, a secret weapon, the Khan's eyes-in-the-sky.

Almost absent-mindedly, Kublai Khan took Haoyou's hand and helped him to his feet. He summoned his physician and told him to tend to the wound in Haoyou's foot. 'Also, find out why he rubs his eye like that.'

'Did the man fall ever into unconsciousness?' enquired the Khan's physician. (He was used to treating the Khan's soldiers who thought of themselves as men by the age of ten.)

'No,' said Mipeng, when no one else had the presence of mind to answer. 'After a bad fall, he did sleep for a long while.'

'Ah!' The doctor, whose abundant silvery hair poured from his head like water overspilling a beaker, closed his eyes and nodded, as if he had won an argument with someone inside his head. 'In this fall, was there a bang to the skull?'

Mipeng and the Miao both looked at Haoyou to answer yes or no. He was unwilling to say: he did not know what he would be letting himself in for. 'I just got mud in my eye,' he said, warily. 'That's all.'

Again the doctor nodded, agreeing with himself. 'And is there ever a light—here—a flickering light?' He waggled his stylus to the left of Haoyou's head, on the very edge of his field of vision.

'No,' said Mipeng, thinking the doctor was asking if lights ever streamed out of her cousin's head.

'No,' said Haoyou. 'No. No. No. No!'

'So very decided!' said the doctor, raising one eyebrow in mild amusement. 'That is strange. I would have expected . . . '

'No. No. No. No. No. No,' said Haoyou, rubbing ferociously at his damaged eye. He would have died sooner than say anything which reduced his father's spirit to an eye affliction, an optical illusion, a flicker of light stealing into the eye because of a bang on the head.

The Khan's physician said that Haoyou's fall into the paddy field, or possibly the repeated whiplash of his head against the kite, had torn part of the eye loose from its socket. They did not understand much that he said, for all he used a slow, deliberate voice he thought suited to illiterate peasants.

But they understood him when he said there must be no more bangs or shocks to the head. They understood all too well his final prognosis: 'Either the eye will mend, or the loss of sight will become total. It is beyond my powers to say.'

Haoyou came away from the doctor's tent walking as if he were trying to balance a water jug on his head; eyes front, keeping his head perfectly still and level. For a long while, nobody spoke. The silence was so oppressive that Mipeng felt obliged to say something. 'The Khan was gracious. To offer his own physician? He seems a very clever man.'

'He is Chinese,' said the circus master, as if that were reason enough for cleverness. He was still bewildered to see how the Conqueror surrounded himself with all things Chinese—Chinese art, Chinese medicine, Chinese religions, Chinese ideas. It was as if Kublai felt a real admiration for the civilization he had conquered. And yet and yet . . .

'So clever, to know about the inside of eyes,' said Mipeng, still struggling to break the silence. She looked round in alarm as Miao Jié came to a full stop and crouched down with his hands over his face.

'What have I done?' he groaned. 'What have I done? I've given the enemy a new weapon and I've blinded the boy!'

'Oh, but the Khan won't make him fly, now! Not when he knows . . . ' Even as she said it, Mipeng knew it was foolish wishful thinking. Haoyou's usefulness as the Khan's 'eyes-in-the-sky' was all that had saved his life. She crouched down beside the circus master, putting her hands over his.

Embarrassed, Haoyou hopped on his one good foot. 'I'm *not* blind!' he said. One knuckle rose, by habit, to his eye, but he stopped short, remembering. 'I want to stay with the circus,' he said, but he could see from the way they looked at him that he had no option. 'I don't *want* to fly for the Khan!' No option, again. 'It wasn't your fault, master,' said Haoyou dismally. 'It was Uncle Bo's fault, not yours.'

The mention of Bo seemed to give the Miao an idea. His face emerged from behind his hands. 'That's it! You can go with them! I told Gou Bo to pack up and go: he'll be leaving right now! If we put you in his baggage, they can turn the circus inside out looking for you . . . my people won't be implicated and you won't be found!'

Haoyou did not want to be one of the bundles among his uncle's baggage. But the Miao was so intent on depriving the Khan of his battle kite, and Mipeng was so intent on saving Haoyou's sight, that between them he had no say.

They found Uncle Bo seated like a Buddha in contemplation, while Auntie Mo sewed his belongings into a piece of cloth which, from now on, she would have to lug on her back. Tears scurried like silver-fish down the lines of her face, but Uncle Bo had his eyes shut too tight to see. He was concentrating all his efforts on self pity. Now and then he would groan and shift his weight from one haunch to the other, and say, 'Two hundred tael! Two hundred!'

'You need not trouble with that, Madam Gou Mo,' said the circus master running up to her and taking the bundle out of her arms. 'You may take the smallest of the wagons—and rice enough to last a month. Here! Here are 20 tael to see you home to the coast.'

Auntie Mo was astonishèd. She took the coins, hid them at once in her clothing, and shot a fearful glance in the direction of her husband, knowing he would demand them from her afterwards. 'You are generous, Miao Jié,' she whispered, as if the fat little Buddha were asleep rather than sulking.

'All you have to do in return is to smuggle Haoyou safely out of here.'

The Buddha's eyes opened. 'Nonsense! He's the Khan's man now! A soldier! With me to advise him, his fortune's made! We have no need of your penny-grudging charity now, Miao Jié. *We* shall be travelling with the army!' Self-satisfaction spread over Bo's face, like butter over an egg.

'But, Uncle!' Haoyou was shocked. 'We'd be fighting for the Khan! Against Chinese, maybe! Against the True Emperor!' (He shot an embarrassed glance at the Miao.)

Bo shrugged and jutted his lower lip so far forward that it looked like the spout of an oil jar. 'Who are you to judge your betters?'

'But, Uncle!' Mipeng knelt down where she was and

pressed her palms together. 'The truth is, Haoyou must not fly any more. The Royal Physician says his eye is damaged. If he bangs his head, he may lose his sight in that eye. So . . . '

Uncle Bo lurched up from the floor, like a whale breaching, and lifted the flat of his hand. 'So if I box his ears, he will have no more reason to hesitate?'

Auntie Mo's sewing hands paused trembling over the bundle of belongings. First her husband had taken her away from Dagu and her home, then among elephants and barbarians, sleeping in tents and on boats. Now she was to be conscripted into the army of Kublai Khan, among thick-browed women who carried swords and rode into battle, and rattled their old bones about on horseback until they fell into spillikins. 'That boy Chiggis . . . ' she said tentatively. (She had to say it twice before she was heard.) 'That boy on the blue kite . . . '

'What about him?' snapped Bo.

'I heard . . . I heard his family were looking for you, honoured husband. Wanting blood money. Or revenge. I'm not sure. If we stay they will come and find us and . . . ' Her voice tailed away. She kept her eyes determinedly on her sewing.

Haoyou wished she would look up, so he could show her, with a smile, how very, very grateful he was to her for the lie.

An hour later, Bo and Mo were perched up on the front of a little bullock cart which had once held Bukhur's birdcages. Haoyou climbed into the sack which was to conceal him as the cart left camp. Only now did it occur to him that he and his cousin were about to part company with the Jade Circus for ever. The Miao was trying to fold the sacking over his head, but he kept bobbing up again, filled with regrets and questions. 'What will happen to the kite? Will you get some other boy to fly it?'

'It is already the Khan's property,' said Miao Jié. 'Now stay quiet.'

Haoyou crouched down, but almost at once bobbed up again. 'I wouldn't have minded! My eye, I mean. If I could have gone on flying for you!'

Miao smiled a crooked, wistful smile. 'My conscience can only bear so much, Sun Swallow.'

'I'm Phoenix now. You forgot. I got bigger than a swallow. I'm Phoenix.'

The Miao laid a hand on his head to persuade him back into the sack, but his hand simply rested there, ruffling Haoyou's hair. 'Myself, I would choose the swallow's life every time. Nothing but sunlight and blue skies, and no need to go into the fire.'

Haoyou felt a strong desire to fling his arms around the circus master. But how can a sailor's son hug a member of the Imperial Chinese Family? He had to settle for saying, 'I don't want to go. I liked being Sun Swallow. You . . . People were good to Sun Swallow.'

The Miao briskly pulled up the sides of the sack and used a piece of cord to tie it shut. 'There is one service you can do me, friend,' he said in a low voice. 'Never repeat the things I told you. About my history. It is just that: history. And it might make trouble for the Jade Circus. Do you understand?'

A muffled promise came from inside the sack. 'Never! I wouldn't! Never!'

Miao Jié picked up the sack and carried it over his shoulder to the cart, setting it down between a bag of rice and three sleeping rolls.

'Get up, Mipeng,' said Auntie Mo. 'You are keeping your uncle waiting.'

'I am not going,'

Inside his sack, Haoyou felt his heart turn as slippery and cold as a fish on a slab.

'You are delaying me, girl. Get into the cart,' Bo commanded.

'I cannot. My place is here. With Miao Jié.'

Bo puffed and snorted and gave a laugh so malicious that his mouth actually turned downwards. 'I regret to disappoint you, Miss, but the Gou family has been dismissed by Great Circus Cat there. *We are not wanted.*'

Haoyou stretched the sacking tight with both hands, trying to peer out. He saw indistinctly two shapes merge, as Miao Jié put an arm around Mipeng. 'As to that, sir, rest content. She is wanted. In fact, I have to come to rely on her good advice and company.'

Through the open-weave of the sack, Haoyou saw, as a medium must see—dark, looming shapes, blurred but unmistakable: things he ought to have seen months before. Of course! It was all plain now. He had thought the Miao was confiding in him, Haoyou. But he had only been talking to Mipeng—a conversation between sweethearts—allowing her little cousin to sit in, because he was small and harmless.

Jealousy, like a badly lit firework, fizzled and fumed in Haoyou's guts. He did not even know whether he was jealous of Mipeng or Miao Jié. Between them, they had robbed him of his only friends in the world.

'You are a disgrace to the family name of Gou,' said Uncle Bo in his most ponderous and portentous voice. 'Never show yourself again in Dagu. Our door is shut to you.'

Haoyou did not realize the cart had jolted into movement: he thought his heart had bruised him by pitching around his chest. As the little bullock cart trundled out through the squalor of the Jade Circus, he glimpsed, through the sacking, the damaged red kite flapping against its prop, like a big red heart pulsing.

He had not been able to say goodbye to Bukhur or the baby named after him; to the roustabouts who had towed him into the sky, to the riders who had caught him out of it! He had forgotten to give a titbit to the tiger, or fulfil the dare he had dared himself: to stand just once on the elephant's knobbly head. He never would learn now how to walk a tightrope or milk a horse or swallow fire. He would never again fly into the blue country, mountainous with clouds, where the spirits live on for ever. Never see Mipeng again.

Fright kept his tears in check for a while: the Khan's outriders looked over the cart and asked where Bo was heading. But they knew of the bet and how Bo had lost it; they knew his reasons for leaving. They had only stopped him because they wanted a chance to smirk at him and his ugly wife and make jokes in Mongol at his expense. They saw no kite in the cart, so did not look for the kite-boy.

Then the bullock cart was alone, following one of the Khan's mail roads, heading east. Haoyou gave himself up to crying—a thing he had not done when his house burned, when Bo beat him, when his shoulder broke, when the Khan's bodyguard rested a foot on his back. He was still crying when Bo tugged open the neck of the sack and told him to take a turn at the reins. 'What are you snivelling for?'

But Haoyou did not seem able to stop the tears which came splashing like the first raindrops of the monsoon, making big round marks on the silk of his red costume. They ached in such quantities behind his eyes that he feared they would wash the torn eye out of its socket and blind him then and there; still he could not stop crying. His uncle slapped at his shoulders and the arms he held up to protect his head.

'Look at you! First you ruin me, and then you see to it

that we're turned out into a wilderness a thousand miles from home—bandits . . . starvation . . . ' Bo was pummelling his body now, with small fat fists. 'The gods sent you as a plague upon me! As for that girl!'

'Don't even speak her name, husband!' Auntie Mo chimed in. 'She dirties the earth she walks on! To think a girl of the Gou family would lower herself to consort with a circus gypsy!'

'He's not a gypsy!' protested Haoyou, turning away and stooping, so as to shield his head. 'Don't! You wouldn't say that if you knew!'

'I should have strangled her then and there, in front of her *gypsy*, pah! I would have been within my rights to strangle her, disobedient hussy!'

'You should, husband. Indeed, you should! . . . "Miao Mipeng".' (She tasted Mipeng's married name as if it were curdled milk.)

'—And that's all supposing he marries her!'

'I shall see to it her name is wiped away like chalk off a slate!' (Husband and wife warmed to their theme.) 'Miao Mipoo-pah!'

'But it isn't!' retorted Haoyou. A red haze of rage had risen up, blinding him more completely than any bang on the head. 'You should be proud! For Mipeng to be loved by a man like him!'

'A man like what?' sneered Uncle Bo. 'The "Little Miao"? The *Miniature* Miao? King of the Beggars?'

'He's not! He's not! He's not!' raged Haoyou. 'He's better than you! He's better than any of you! He's only a Song nobleman, that's all! He's only a member of the Song royal family!'

Even then, his promise did not rise up and plug his mouth. When Uncle Bo laughed, Haoyou went on and on trying to silence him, telling more and more, spilling out every fact he knew about Miao Jié's Imperial connections, his odd spiritual pilgrimage, his quest to look Kublai Khan in the eye.

Haoyou did not tell it well, but that did not matter. Bo gleaned all the facts he needed . . . Meanwhile, Auntie Mo leaned back into the cart fanning herself with the fly whisk. 'Fancy! Gou Mipeng the medium, married to royalty!'

Uncle Bo struggled back on to the front of the cart and, slashing at the bullocks with the goad, drove them in a great circle.

'Where are we going?' said Haoyou, having to run so as not to be left behind, clambering on over the tailboard.

'To enter into a very profitable new line of business,' Bo croaked.

Auntie Mo, abandoning her attack of the vapours, sat up. The cart bucked over its own wheel ruts. 'Husband? Oh please, Bo! Do let us get away—far away!'

Uncle Bo smacked his lips like a toad which has just eaten a dragonfly. 'To know your enemy's secrets is to triumph over him. Don't you know that, wife? And I'm just about to triumph over mine!'

18

The Carpet

The army had virtually struck camp by the time they got back. The advance guard had already moved off.

'You're too late!' hissed Haoyou, hidden once more in his sack. 'You're too late!'

But the Khan's tent still stood where it had. The milk-white mares still grazed around its skirts. Kublai had not yet gone, and the circus, although all packed up, awaited his permission to move off in the opposite direction from the army.

Bo drove straight up to the circus master, belligerent as a billy goat, brave because he was sitting higher than Miao Jié's head.

'*What are you doing here?*' called Mipeng, running back from the animal cages when she caught sight of the cart. 'Where's Haoyou? Why have you come back?'

But something about the thrust of Bo's head, the triumphant grin, the malicious gleam in his eye told the Miao everything that had happened.

'I've got your measure, gypsy!' Bo jeered. 'Shall I tell you what's going to happen now? Shall I? Now you're going to sign over the Jade Circus to me! Total ownership! One hundred per cent of the profits!'

Miao Jié slowly blinked his eyes. 'And why would I do that?'

'Because if you don't, I'll tell the Khan who you are and how you came here to assassinate him!'

Haoyou, distraught, burst out of hiding. '*I didn't mean to!*

I didn't know what I was saying!' He said it over and over again. Mipeng looked straight through him, stony, as if he were no one she knew or cared about. Her hand felt for the reassurance of her sweetheart's, but Miao Jié was a stalactite, an icicle, a soul trapped beneath the surface of a frozen lake.

Uncle Bo, on the other hand, was drunk on power and greedy malice. 'What does a member of the House of Song want with a circus in any case? Eh? Tell you what: you may have this little cart,' he said, imitating Miao's refined southern accent, giggling. 'Enough rice to last you a month. Give him twenty cashes, wife. That should see him on his way!'

Auntie Mo looked like a flag tangled round its own post. She was appalled at having returned to the camp of Kublai Khan. She was appalled by her husband's treachery towards a member of the Royal Household. She was ashamed to be linked to this fat, unpatriotic brute by the indissoluble bands of marriage which made all his sins hers too.

'Don't, Bo. Don't,' she kept saying, but not so loud as to risk him hearing her.

'I've watched and learned, watched and learned,' swaggered Bo. 'I see where improvements could be made—savings. Of course there's no reason why you should have a gift for business, is there, Song Jié? You weren't born to it!'

'Please, Bo. Please!' whispered Auntie Mo.

The circus master looked clean through him. Haoyou, sitting curled up on the cart, his arms over his head, wished he were Chiggis dead in his tree rather than Haoyou the traitor, the leaker of secrets, the breaker of promises. *'He called you a gypsy! He said Mipeng was . . . '* But he knew that nothing excused what he had done. Besides, no one was listening.

Very deliberately, and without a word, the Miao held

up his white whip in both hands—a false horizon in front of his eyes. Then he brought it down and broke it across his knee. Picking up his white jacket with inlaid pictures of flowers and beasts, he slipped it on, then turned on his heel and walked away, towards the noisy upheaval of the army breaking camp.

'Where are you going?' called Bo.

The Miao turned and regarded him, like a Buddhist regarding meat. 'I am going to introduce myself to Kublai the Khan. I would sooner die at his hands than live in yours. And I would sooner disband the Jade Circus than entrust it to a man of your . . . *breed.*'

No one went after him. Uncle Bo did not believe he would do it. Everyone else was rooted to the spot by fright and unhappiness.

The Mongol face is inexpressive at the best of times. The face of a Mongol statesman gives absolutely no hint as to the emotions behind it. Kublai Khan received the news from Miao Jié with unperturbed calm.

'So. You offer me surrender. Yes?'

'Surrender?' The idea took Miao Jié by surprise. 'No.'

'You come here to spy on me?'

The Miao inclined his head to one side. 'No.'

They stood face-to-face, expressionless, discussing life and death.

'To kill me?'

'I often thought of it, but . . . Nights past number, I thought of it. My father's spirit urged me to it.'

'I remember your father,' said the Khan. 'A very stiff-necked man.'

'You broke that stiff neck under your horses' hooves. You rolled him in a carpet and had him trampled to death.'

Behind the Khan, his travelling pavilion was being dismantled. The great central post was taken away, and the tent's roof sank down with a sigh. The out-rush of air blew Miao's hair away from his face. Before the side poles could be removed, the silk-woven carpet which lay on the ground had to be deftly rolled up by four soldiers on their knees.

'And now you seek a carpet of your own, do you?' said the Khan. 'You interest me, man of Song. I have a rebellion to put down, or we could talk more. Maybe you began it, this rebellion? Yes? No? I have seen it often: you Chinese, you call Death to you. Like cows at milking time, you call Death to you.' He said something to the men dismantling his tent, and they brought the carpet and unrolled it again at his feet. 'Royal blood should not spill on the ground. All my life I have held to this most strongly. That is why I never cut the heads off princes. In my own family; in yours. Not emperors, not princes, not kinsmen.'

The noisy confusion of the campsite had gradually died away, as word spread that a Song assassin had been discovered, unmasked, and stood now in front of the Khan, awaiting execution. A tightly packed ring of Mongol and Chinese faces—both army and circus—gathered to watch: the ultimate spectacle.

The surface of the carpet glistened, silvery as water, its subtle pattern of leaves and animals hard to see in the bright sunlight. When the Khan gave the command for his horsemen to mount up, the crowd on the opposite side of the impromptu arena quickly drew aside. Soon the horses would be riding to and fro at full gallop across the space of ground; it would not be safe to get in their way. To and fro, to and fro they would ride, across the rolled-up carpet, hooves striking the delicate warp and weft, until carpet and contents were nothing but a flattened, shapeless mound.

The Great Miao lay down on the carpet's edge and the Khan regarded him for a long moment with his sharp, hawkish eyes. He poked a slippered foot under the carpet's fringing and winced, troubled by a touch of gout. Then he flicked the carpet's edge over Miao Jié's body. His riders began to whistle and yelp—the odd, animal-like noises of pent-up blood lust. The four soldiers went down on their knees again, to roll the carpet up, this time with a member of the Imperial Song family inside.

'Wait!' It was Mipeng. She pushed her way through the press of onlookers and walked over to the carpet. 'You are wrong. Song Jié never meant to harm you. He is not his father. He came here to see what kind of man had conquered his country.' Then she lay down alongside Miao Jié.

Haoyou, forgetting he was in hiding, rose up on the top of the cart. The blood roared so fast through his head that it pulsed in his damaged eye and let in a shape like a running figure. But he took no notice. He knew if he moved fast enough that his heart would not have time to break. The fear he was used to. This was no more than falling out of the sky, after all.

The flickering figure kept pace with him as he jumped down from the cart and ran towards the grey carpet to lie down beside Mipeng. The softness of the pile, the intricacy of the design, the various food and drink stains all impressed themselves so vividly that he was scarcely aware of the flicker in his eyes. Through the fingertips of one hand, he could feel the skin of Mipeng's arm, cold as snow. Through the other, he felt the threadbare softness of Little Dog Wu. Through the carpet he could feel the judder made by the Mongol cavalry, trampling hooves impatient to be moving.

Then he felt a row of buttons blip his arm, and found the great bulk of the Szechwan clown lowering itself into place alongside him. The big, lugubrious face still wore its grinning make-up.

After the clown came two dancers, and after them the ribbon twirler. With a hollow knocking, a pair of yellow stilts, leant against a cart, fell over all by themselves. Their owner was just then stretching himself out on the Khan's silken carpet. The crowd's murmuring rose like an incoming tide. Soon only the fringes of silver grey were visible, so many people lay side by side across its length.

When Bukhur the bird-catcher came, baby son in his arms, there were gasps of astonishment from the Khan's army, but his example brought other Jade Circus Mongols—riders and roustabouts, young men and boys, a woman in a blue veil. They pushed and jostled each other for room aboard that grey silk raft bound for Eternity.

Left all alone by the bullock cart, Uncle Bo stared open-mouthed as the Jade Circus—*his* Jade Circus—expressed its devotion to the man in the white jacket, and migrated wholesale into the path of the Mongol cavalry. When the thin, ugly woman beside him also began to move forward, he snatched hold of her arm—'Are you mad, woman?'—and pinned Mo tightly in her place beside him. The next time the crowd surged closed in front of him, Bo dragged his wife into the bullock cart and drove away, not caring which way he went or what he took with him, just anxious to be somewhere else when the Jade Circus was massacred. He nursed the bitter impression that the gods had set out expressly to thwart and disappoint him. How else could he have started the day with such high hopes and twice seen his fortunes dashed?

Haoyou lay between the clown and the medium and listened to the sound of his heart beating. He heard the rattle of a bullock cart, the hiss of a forge extinguished. He heard Kublai give an order in Mongol, and start to laugh.

174

He braced himself and looked up at the blue sky, expecting to see it fill with flying hooves.

But although the cavalry broke into a gallop, the drum of hooves receded into the distance. The Khan's laughter also moved off.

A face bent into Haoyou's field of vision, black against the brightness of the sky. It was the Urghal warrior who had been put in charge of the Khan's newest weapon. Having loaded the kite on to a cart, he had come now in search of the kite's rider.

As Haoyou got up, Bukhur's oldest son also rose shakily to his feet and went and folded the carpet edge reverently back off his master's face. 'The Khan gone, master,' he said. 'The Khan is merciful.'

The Great Miao passed a hand over his face and stood up. He looked at the colourful array of bodies lying like a logjam from end to end, edge to edge of the grey carpet and far beyond. They looked back at him, blinking, smiling shyly. Bukhur's baby kicked its feet in the air and sent a yellow jet of water high into the air.

'*Goodbye, master! Goodbye, Mipeng! Goodbye, everyone!*'

Miao Jié spun round in time to see his kite-boy, seated pillion on a Tartar horse, looking back for as long as the horse's jolting let him, waving and waving his regretful goodbyes: a weapon now in the Khan's army.

19
Weapon of War

After the unexpected contact with their ancestors, the people of Yangcun did not let their relations slide back into airy oblivion. Haoyou and his 'translator', Tongue of Fire had turned Yangcun into a town of devout and fervid worshippers. Ever since the Jade Circus left, they had been sending messages and presents of tea, spices, medallions, and rice paper notes up into the sky, attached to the legs of pigeons. The slightest thing to drop out of the sky, therefore, took on a magical significance and was held to have been sent by the spirits. Kites flew all day over the sluggish river—not manned kites, of course, but little ornamental ones with prayers for the dead attached, or questions from the living:

'Where is the cat?'

'Who stole my hoe?'

'How am I going to endure your mother?'

When the kites did not come down again annotated with messages, the people of Yangcun did not start to question whether their ancestors were up there, or suspect the circus had in some way tricked them. No, they examined their kites with microscopic scrutiny and interpreted every little rip and rain streak as a message from the spirit world. They interpreted the way the kites flew and how willingly they came back to earth.

Naturally 'experts' emerged in this business of interpreting spirit messages: kite-readers, mediums. Before long, Yangcun believed it was in daily two-way communication with the spirit world.

This might not in itself have mattered, if politics had not entered in. But the old men at the gaming tables, began saying (as old men do) that the northern provinces should never have been lost to the Conquerors, that the young men had not fought hard enough. Previously, they and the young men would have argued, then let the matter drop until another day. But now they had the spirits overhead to decide such arguments, didn't they? They sent up two kites: one white for peace, one red for war, and asked the spirits whether they ought to rise up in rebellion against Kublai Khan.

The red one accidentally smashed the white to matchwood.

Into this town, grown sulky and reckless with bravado, rode a detachment of Mongol warriors en route for Korea and the imminent invasion of Japan. Instead of the usual wary respect they expected, they met with an odd hospitality in the form of three barrels of rice wine. It was only after they had drunk it all that they realized: the rice wine had been rather ineffectively poisoned with toadstools.

Five thousand men continued on their way to Korea clutching their stomachs and cursing the people of Yangcun, but too sick to take reprisals. Instead, they informed the Khan by letter, and left it to him to exact punishment on the poisoners of Yangcun.

And here he was to exact it.

It was with a horrible foreboding that Haoyou recognized the river scenery where he had had prayers tied to his hair, tea posted into his mouth, and rice tipped down his trouser legs. The unhappiness he would have felt at fighting against anyone Chinese was made ten times worse by the fact that he *knew* these people, had met these people, had fooled and tricked and taken money from them because they were too solemn to enjoy a straightforward circus.

What would Mipeng have said? What would The Great Miao have told him to do? A few weeks ago, thought Haoyou, it would have been easier: he would simply have done whatever he was told. 'Obedient to the last.' 'A good obedient boy.' That was all the praise he had ever looked for. But since joining the Jade Circus, even Obedience did not seem to leave a boy in the clear.

And he was lonelier than he had ever been in his life. Kublai Khan was magnificent and spellbinding. Twice he had spared Haoyou's life. But did that make him a friend? Hardly. His tent was a distant banner and a sprinkling of white horses.

It was not simply that Haoyou found himself living among Mongols: (Bukhur would have been almost as welcome a sight as Wawa or the sweet-cake maker in Dagu). But the few words Bukhur had taught him hardly equipped him to make friends. 'Nice horse' was about the best he could manage. It no longer irked him that they dropped their trousers in public: you can get used to anything in time. But the *tajik* in him—the keeper-to-one-place—wanted to go home, craved to go home, longed to see a familiar face, house, or view. Not *one* of these men could understand such a feeling (even if Haoyou were able to express it). What these warriors wanted was the next good fight, the next chance to get blind drunk, to see over the next horizon.

Just once, for the fun of it, they had sent Haoyou up into the sky, and the swaggering knights with their gerfalcons on their wrists had loosed their birds to see what would happen. Some of the hawks had settled to the ground, uneasy under the shadow of the kite. Others had circled at a respectful distance. But one had lunged at him, like a moth at a flame, hooked feet splayed, beak slashing, and had cut a scar in Haoyou's cheek before falling away down the sky, whistling.

* * *

The weather turned very strange as they came within sight of Yangcun. A high wind began to pull the clouds about, like the Mongols when they played polo with a dead goat.

The people of Yangcun, learning of the Mongols' coming, began building barricades across the road, piling up carts, rice, sacks, bags of river mud.

The wind, too, as if in imitation of them, began piling up barricades of cloud—big black woolsacks of cloud, tuffets and mattresses and carpets of cloud piled up against a wall of flinty sky.

The straggle of warriors (who never observed any military discipline between battles) also began to close ranks, their shaggy, mailed-sheepskin waistcoats merging into a fleecy-edged blackness, the noise of their horses' hooves into a single thunderous rumble.

There would be no need to wait for the lumbering war-machines to catch up. One swift cavalry charge, a few firebrands tossed on to a few roofs, the summary killing of anyone found out of doors, the swift despatch of the town's officials, should be enough to restore public order. There might even be a glimpse of the Mighty Khan himself, riding enthroned upon four elephants to receive the town's plea for mercy.

The Khan did not indulge in wholesale massacres; he was, by the standards of his ancestors, a merciful man. But the biggest empire in the history of the world cannot afford to tolerate rebellion, however puny.

As soon as they saw the dust rising from the Khan's approaching army, the people of Yangcun abandoned their barricades and ran for the newly built temple on the hill. It was not much of a hill, but it was quite a temple, considering the speed with which it had been built. With its flags and dovecotes, mirrors and birdcages, lamps, altars, and white-painted message-boards, it reflected the town's recent obsession with the ancestral spirits overhead. Now, with danger on their doorstep, they summoned help not from their neighbours downriver, but from their dead relations, waving every colour of flag, and blowing whistles night and day, beckoning their allies in the sky.

When he saw their temple, Haoyou was half inclined to despise them. Ever since his interview with the Khan's doctor, he had known better than to put his trust in the spirits. Didn't these fools know that magic was just a circus trick? Didn't they know that the Mongol Dead had probably driven the Chinese Dead out of heaven long ago? Didn't they realize by now that the spirits do not show themselves? Only tricks of the light, optical illusions.

Kublai Khan could easily have sent sappers to undermine the temple, fired burning arrows into its roofs, shelled it with balls of tar, even charged it down with elephants. But curious to test out his new weapon of war, he gave instructions that the Kite Boy should be sent aloft, to drop packets of explosive on to the temple. If the explosions did not kill the renegades, the fire which followed would drive them out-of-doors where the cavalry could drive them downhill into the brown river.

While the cavalry contented themselves with setting light to parts of the empty town, the rope team prepared the kite and its rider.

'This weather is odd,' said Haoyou, but they did not understand him.

The great red kite, dust-covered again from its journey, flexed and rattled in the rising wind. The trees trembled, as if at some premonition of horror. The animals, too, were uneasy, throwing up their heads, scenting rain. This weather was unseasonable, driving in from the east, bringing seagulls with it from a sea one hundred miles away. And Haoyou had no way of saying, 'I don't like this wind.'

He did not trust the rope team who had flown Chiggis to his death and now squabbled about how to launch him. (At first they suggested, by gestures, that he climb a tree and jump off it.) He did not trust the spirits to favour him, now that he was tethered, heart-and-hide, to the Mongols. In fact he did not rate his chances very highly at all.

When they gave him the bombs to carry, he knew he had come to the end of his glory days.

The team had no grasp of how kites worked—of how difficult it would be for him to hold anything, let alone parcels of explosive dangling lit tallow fuses. He had no means of explaining how inflammable the kite was, that the fuses would not hang straight down, that it was not a ship he could steer wherever they wanted it to go. Haoyou wanted to tell them it could not be done.

But just as the first drops of rain began to fall, the rope team paid out the rope, arrayed themselves along it, and began to tow him over the flat ground.

'Oi!' he said, starting to run, bent under the weight of the kite, the fuses dancing round his feet. 'Not like that!' But then he was on his knees, on his stomach, being towed over the ground, while the big kite flopped and banged above him like a runaway wagon running him over. Pebbles embedded themselves in his knees. The erratic breeze picked up the kite only to slam it down again. The rope team, angry now, came and picked up both kite and boy.

'You need a *hill*!' he yelled at them. 'You need a *high place*!' But they only cursed him in their own language and tried throwing him into the air like a paper dart. This time he collided with a tree, and several twigs poked through the red silk. '*A hill*!' he bawled. '*High ground*!'

They ran off to seek advice, abandoning Haoyou in his tree. He seized the opportunity to pinch out the fuses.

If only someone like the Miao were there, as a go-between, everything might still be cleared up without a full-scale battle. But there was no Miao, and the rain was coming on harder, muddying everything.

The rope team came back with still more men, thinking brute strength was the answer. Seeing the dead fuses, they ran and fetched torches. They were all jabbering excitedly, and kept looking at the sky, which was darkening to the colour of an old bruise. In their clumsy, bungling haste, they not only re-lit the fuses, but two or three of the dangling bamboo whistles. Haoyou tried to tell them, but it was futile.

All of a sudden, a great gust of cold air was sucked in under the black clouds, as if the river were catching its breath. It lifted Haoyou miraculously upwards, through no effort of the rope team who were left gaping for a few moments before they snatched violently at the rope. Haoyou's body cracked like a whip, and light burst in at the side of his head.

The fuses came licking up between his legs, stinging like wasps. The bamboo whistles, dry and hollow, burned in musical harmony, eerily loud. Black circular scorches appeared in Haoyou's silk. He might have heard himself scream but for the first clap of thunder.

At the noise of the thunderclap, half the team dropped the rope and ran back the way they had come. The rest heaved and hauled, paid out and drew in, recalling now things they had been shown by the circus hands.

When Haoyou saw the bright figure of a running man out of the corner of his left eye, he could not imagine why he had ever mistaken it for his father. Gou Pei had been a little, undernourished man stunted by injury and bad food. He would never have translated into this golden sprinter. This was no more than light leaking into his brain. An eyeful of lightning.

When Haoyou heard the voice inside his head, speaking his name, speaking the names of his mother and Wawa, saying, *'When I get home this time . . . When I get home . . .'* Haoyou knew he was remembering, just remembering.

But he looked about him anyway, head aching, neck rigid, and found himself in a country beyond his most wild imaginings. Capes and isthmuses of cloud supported a jet black kingdom of cloud taller than any mountain range. Caverns yawned alongside hanging gardens and palaces a thousand storeys high. Sudden portals opened and released streamers of solid gold, as if the gods themselves were imprisoned inside. A sea of cloud rolled in and broke in slow motion against these titanic cloud bases. Faces formed, but faces miles high and changing their expressions by the second; their mouths drained the white out of neighbouring clouds, leaving them black as tar pits. The whole perimeter of the sky seemed to begin revolving, while the valley below was hit by an onrush of wind all the way from the sea, tasting of salt and pitch and cormorants.

Haoyou felt a force seize the kite like none he had ever felt before. The wind filled his lungs without him even needing to breathe. He saw the thin, painted panels ripped from the sides of the hilltop temple; flying away like birds. Lightning made the black landscape bright as day, then the thunder cracked it such a blow that buildings and trees flinched in the shock-wave. The wind was so solid, he was sure he could walk on it without the aid of a kite.

Haoyou thought it was the end of the world. His rope trailed below him like the umbilical cord of a baby stolen away by the gods, ripped from its mother's grasp at the moment of birth.

Meanwhile, a red glow crept up the fuses of his explosive packages. The burned out whistles flew by him, like black owl pellets—there seemed to be no gravity to carry them downwards—but the fuses still burned, closer and closer. Soon the kite would blossom into a single scarlet bloom and turn to ash, consuming Haoyou as it did so.

He saw the temple beneath him, its roof-beam ends curved upwards to repel demons, and realized, with a shock, that he, Haoyou, was just that—a demon, a sky demon, a winged bringer of death.

With a cry, Haoyou also realized he was still holding the bombs. Waiting for age-long seconds, he held them until the temple was behind him and empty countryside below, then threw both away from him with all his might.

They came back at him on the wind—weightless in the wind—and bumped into his face before spinning away. The twin explosions were silent, swallowed up by another drum roll of thunder, but he felt them like a single blow from a stick. And in the selfsame moment, the fire reached the face of the kite—flammable silk caked with flammable glue.

Below him, the Mongols sacking Yangcun, who feared nothing but the gods and lightning, took to their heels and fled. They did not stop running until they reached the supply wagons. Then they dragged their yurts off the luggage wagons and rolled themselves in the folds of hide, shutting out the noise, shutting out the light, shutting out all but the terror which was so great that they were not even ashamed to show it. Their gods were angry, and while the storm raged, there was nothing to be done but to hide as completely as possible from the eyes of heaven.

The storm, born a thousand miles away at sea, took no sides between Mongol and Chinese. It picked the nails out of the ancestral temple and demolished it, flag by mirror by birdcage. Like insects fleeing a termite hill, people spilled from the base and scattered in all directions. Such a storm might have been sent by their ancestors, to save them from the Mongols, but if so, why were the lightning bolts striking town and why was the rain filling the river, minute by minute, to bursting point?

Haoyou also saw the river fill: like a snake swallowing a rat, its whole brown shape bulged. Its surface was rough as a grater, with the intensity of the rain.

Rain! The noise of its drumming on the silk was deafening. The fire that licked around the frame's base went out with a hiss—'Oh, thank you, Father!'—but the weight of the silk suddenly doubled. Within seconds, every cord, every strut, every gutter and seam was saturated. He dropped with a flop-flopping motion, like a seal slapping its way over rocks. And as he fell, the fortresses of cloud around him pounded one another with flame-throwers of sodium yellow lightning, with saltpetre thunder. The electrical charge in the air was so intense that the kite glowed with static: a blue incandescence.

When Haoyou could neither see for the glare, nor hear for the thunder, *that* was when he knew his father was nearby—not a fiery, running figure, not some celestial seraph armed with fistfuls of helpful magic—just *there*.

As all the Dead are there, a breath away, always.

Like Icarus he plunged into the river—a brown foaming hardness which felt as solid as sunbaked earth. Its swollen waters clutched the kite and swept it, circling, downstream, breaking it into smaller and smaller pieces. The fragments merely clung together as people do, in adversity.

20

Half-light

The storm which smashed Yangcun was a cloudburst in comparison with the typhoon which had spawned it. Born far out in the China Seas, it was almost spent by the time it reached Yangcun, deep inland. Hours beforehand, Kublai Khan's invasion force, poised to add Japan to their conquests, had been scattered, broken by it, sunk by waves the size of mountains. Twenty thousand invasion troops ran back to their ships and put out to sea, thinking it the best place to weather a typhoon. Out of twelve hundred vessels to set sail, mere dozens stayed afloat, limping home, like smashed kites, to the Korean coast. Their crews were half mad, talking of water-dragons and sky-hounds and gods who could roll up the sea like a carpet.

Alongside such a catastrophe, Yangcun shrank to nothing. Besides, after the river burst and the banks were flooded, the river basin was no longer a fit place for a battle. It was a quagmire, half awash with the litter of broken buildings, drowned animals, sodden yurts. The Mongols, emerging from their hiding places, wondered what they had done to deserve such a scare, and were more eager to propitiate their angry ancestors than fight a few misguided zealots. Kublai Khan was deeply shaken when news arrived, by a relay of postal ponies, of his fleet's destruction. It was the greatest defeat of his career and he cursed himself for not tackling the capture of Japan in person. His mind was swept clean of minor rebellions, of electric storms, of kite-boys. If ever he remembered the experiment, while kneeling before his altar of Steppes grass and soil, it was only for long enough to observe, 'I knew it would never work.'

He saw no use in sending anyone to look for the kite's wreckage, the kite-boy's body.

When Haoyou surfaced in the swollen, boiling river, there was no sign of his kite. He still wore his harness, but the panels had been stripped away, broken, unglued and crumpled into litter which spun downriver along with tons of other debris. A dead goat butted Haoyou in the face; he shoved it away, revolted, and struggled to disentangle himself from the harness.

A table, a shoe, a basket.

If the rope caught on the river bed, he would be dragged underwater and drowned. He was not swimming: there was no point in swimming in such a current: the water simply rolled him over and over until he was so exhausted he could scarcely judge when his head was above water and when it was below.

An oar, a length of cord, a wine bladder.

There washed into his head a story he had heard—who from?—about the battle of Dali when Kublai Khan's troops had crossed the Qinxa river using sheepskin bags to keep afloat. He grabbed the wine bladder and tried to cling on, but it was too slimy to hold. After a few moments it slipped out of his hands. A great sheet of wood came circling downstream, spinning so fast that it almost sheared off his head. Fending it off with his hands, he actually managed to pull one arm, one knee over the edge. Spread-eagled on the board, he felt it begin to spin again—a sickening, whirling, see-sawing motion that turned the sky into a vortex of brown, reeling clouds. Only by dipping his feet into the water—using them as a rudder—did he achieve a terrifying forward career down the swollen river. Thuds against the underside of the board might have been rocks or logs or giant sturgeon, river demons or fence posts. His trailing feet grew so cold that he could no longer feel them, but he had clamped himself tight as a barnacle to the board and nothing was going to shift him, not if he had to sail to the sea itself!

The storm died. A dense grey downpour washed it out of the sky, flattened the river, drowned out the thunder. It was a matter of hours before Haoyou realized that the board to which he clung bore Chinese characters and flowers. It was cladding from the walls of the Yangcun temple tower.

Haoyou turned his head to relieve one cheek of the chilling, prickling rain. The sky turned instantly dark. He turned his head back: the sky turned grey. He turned his head again: no sky. Haoyou raised his pointy chin and rested it on the gold brushstrokes of the character meaning 'sky'. To his right he could see the river bank: tree, a house, a water buffalo. To his left: nothing. He turned his head to complete the panorama: rice paddies, a boat jetty, a monastery. He knew now the nature of his surroundings: light to starboard, dark to port. He knew too that he was blind in one eye. Somewhere in the cooling core of his body, he knew it was a blow, a tragedy, a terrible loss. But as for the rest of him, he could not make it matter at all. It was a blackberry stain, a scorchmark, a tiny tear in the stretched white fabric of Life. He was alive, and all he wanted now was to stay alive. If he could see his mother again, he did not greatly care whether it was with one eye or two.

It was a whole month later that Haoyou reached Dagu on the shore of the China Sea. Working on riverside farms for his supper, cadging rides on downriver boats, he had gradually retraced the route taken by the Jade Circus as it travelled towards Dadu. No one recognized him as Phoenix or Sun Swallow or Qiqi. Without his red wings, he was as common as any caterpillar, and as much of a nuisance.

The ordinariness of Dagu in turn astounded him. It was as if nothing had happened here—no circuses, no battles, no miraculous rescues or insane bets. The Japanese typhoon had left its mark—there were roofs still needing repair, and stones were being shifted back along the beach from where the tide wash had reshaped the bay. But all in all Haoyou could scarcely credit the everyday ordinariness of Dagu Town. A fishing boat was docking. A market was in progress. Two hand-barrows confronted each other at a street corner and their owners squabbled over right of way. It was Paradise.

Haoyou hurried past his burned-out cottage and on up the hill to Uncle Bo's house, where his mother and Wawa would be sitting thinking of him, praying for him, wishing him home again. 'Mama!' he called, running the last few streets, running faster and faster. 'Mama! Wawa!'

The house was empty. Its door and windows were boarded up. Haoyou looked around him. Could he have got the wrong house? Come to the wrong door? He hammered on the nailed-up window, foolish in his panic. He picked up a loose plank of wood and circled the house looking for somewhere he could force his way in. Sneak thieves had long since beaten him to it. Planks dangled loosely from a rear window, and when he climbed in, there was no sign of furniture, or food, of clothing or even a household shrine.

Haoyou contemplated his situation. As far as he knew, the only prospect he had of eating today was the single cash trapped in the lining of his wadding jacket. He sat down with his back to the wall, and worked away at the coin with finger and thumb until it slid round to a ragged seam and popped out. Then, to his bitter rage, it slipped through his fingers, dropped on to the plank-covered floor and rolled away down a crack between two planks. Calling himself and the coin all the names he could think of, he set about prising the planks up, to get back his cash. To his astonishment, the planks came up easily enough, once he had found the finger-holes Uncle Bo had cut in them.

There, underneath, safe from house-breakers and prying eyes, lay a 'cargo-hold' of assorted goods: hanks of raw silk, cakes of incense, tea, buttons, a roll of creamy blank paper, cooking oil, cinnamon sticks, brass spoons, fireworks, cowhide belts, a box of long, carved hairpins, the horn of some kind of animal, fish line, and four bottles of rice wine. A year ago, Haoyou might have thought these were his great-uncle's treasured possessions—family heirlooms, perhaps, or presents for Auntie Mo. Today, Haoyou was in no doubt that these were goods filched from the warehouse where Gou Bo had worked for forty years. Only the prospect of richer pickings (and being fired) had persuaded him to leave Dagu and go in search of the Jade Circus. One thing was sure: as soon as Bo had gambled away the last of his money, he would be back for these ill-gotten savings of his. All Haoyou had to do was wait, and Uncle Bo would be back. But he could not wait until then to find out what had become of his mother and sister. After helping himself to some of the tea and cooking oil, Haoyou replaced the planks, climbed back out, and tried to resecure the window by hammering in the nails with his shoe.

A neighbour stuck her head above the fence. 'No use knocking,' she said. 'Gou Bo is gone, boy. Shut up the house and went. Dadu way.'

'But Gou Qing'an! Little Wawa? Where are they? Where's my mother?' His voice came out high and unhappy.

The neighbour beckoned Haoyou closer to peer at him short-sightedly. Her button nose twitched as if she scented juicy gossip. 'Well, bless me, if it isn't the kite-boy! The one who ran off with the circus.'

'I was apprenticed . . . ' Haoyou began defensively.

'Bo and Mo went off upriver, like I say. Maybe they went looking for you.'

'Yes, yes, they did. They found me. But Mama! Qing'an! She wasn't with them! Great-Uncle said he had "left her in good hands".'

The neighbour tipped her head on one side and twisted her mouth into a grimace. 'Good hands, huh! The gods send him good leeches and bad doctors for that one. "Good hands", indeed!'

The certainty washed over Haoyou that his mother was dead—an epidemic, perhaps, or the typhoon . . . 'What happened?'

'Oooh, boy. I don't like to say . . . '

'*What happened to Mama? Where is she? Where's my sister?*'

'Ah well, you know how he was with his betting, your uncle . . . '

'Betting?'

'Gambling, yes. Well, he needed the money, and the liquor-house needed a what-d'you-call-it, and there was nowhere else for your mother to go. So he signed her over to them. As a what-d'you-call-it? Serving woman. She didn't like to take the little one with her—not to a place like that—well, who would? But she did, and she has, so there it is.'

'What? Where?' Haoyou could feel the tears paining his damaged eye.

'At the liquor-house, like I said.' In stepping down from the fence, the neighbour disappeared from sight. Her voice grew more distant. 'So these parts don't talk about

191

her any more, beauty or not. A woman who works in a place like that . . . '

Her voice drizzled on as Haoyou leapt down from the fence and went running back down the alleyways, splashing through yellow puddles and over rotten fruit, vaulting over fishing pots and chicken coops on down to the quayside to find his mother.

A new warehouse was being built, and it took him a moment to remember where the Don't-Go-Near-House stood in relation to the harbour. When he found it, he ran down the steps to the rotten cellar door which never opened. No one had plugged the hole which Mipeng had pushed through the rotten wood.

When he first put his eye to the hole, Haoyou sobbed aloud with frustration. But when he put his good right eye to the hole, instead, the same dingy room presented itself, the scene so unchanged that it might have been a picture hung on the far side of the door: sepia walls, plumes of candle-smoke, torn mattresses spilling their stuffing. Sprawling drunks, arguing drunks, ranting, singing, mumbling drunks swilling away all the vigour and energy they had ever had. Like flayed animals they lay about, open-eyed, empty-eyed, their brains pickled in raw alcohol. A man stood up and spread his arms as if he were flying, then slumped back on to his haunches and hugged himself, eyes staring unseeing at the door beyond which Haoyou crouched, watching.

Only one thing had changed since the last time he and Mipeng had spied on the detestable Di Chou. The old woman was gone who had tended the bubbling stills, met customers at the foot of the ladder, fetched them their drink, taken their money, bowed to them as they stumbled back into the light of day. Her place had been taken by a much younger woman.

'*Mama! Mama! Mama!*' whispered Haoyou to himself,

his hands spread on the cellar door, fingernails digging deep into the wood.

The lout on the door tried to refuse Haoyou entry. It was not his age they objected to, but the fact that he was clearly a penniless rag of a boy. 'I've come to get my father,' said Haoyou. 'He has a boat to catch,' and he was down the ladder before anyone could stop him.

His mother stared at him blankly for a long while, as if trying to put a name to a familiar face.

'Good day, honoured Mother,' said Haoyou. 'Are you well?'

Her fragile beauty, only bruised by the death of her husband, had barely survived life at the drinking den. She was thin, and her hair was grizzled grey.

'I tend animals in a zoo,' she told Haoyou, shrugging helplessly. 'Sometimes they bite. Mostly they are too sleepy.'

'But what happened to the money I sent? The money in the mud ball?'

She shrugged again: thin, hollow collarbones. 'Uncle Bo gambled it away, of course. Can't be helped. But I knew you were doing well—getting rich.' Her eyes wandered over Haoyou's filthy raggedness, unable to reconcile one fact with the other. Along with the fumes bubbling off the stills, she had inhaled all the helplessness of the customers she served, their indifference to whether they lived or died. But her hand gripped his wrist like a vice and would not let go. She looked at him as if he were a ghost which might melt away at any moment.

'And Wawa?' asked Haoyou. He had to coax information out of her a piece at a time, like a baby bird prodding at its mother's beak.

'I keep her safe! I keep her away from the drunks!' she cried defensively. 'We have a little alcove where we sleep—up near the roof. I keep her fed! I keep her clean!' Again her eyes trailed over Haoyou's dirty rags of clothing.

'Good. Good. That's good,' said Haoyou soothingly, trying to extricate his hand. It was hard to be soothing when, inwardly, he was boiling pitch. He wanted to kill Bo, to feed him dice and coins and counters and betting tokens until he choked on them. 'Now you go and get her and pack your things, Mama. You're coming away with me.'

Qing'an drew back against the wall, eyes round. 'Go out? I'm not allowed to go out. Not while there are customers!' For four months she had not stepped out of doors. For four months she had lived in the twilight haze of the cellar, not permitted to leave and having no excuse to even try. Her only pay was food and shelter, though, by the look of her, she had cost the proprietor very little in the way of food.

'Where would we go? I have nothing. We have nothing.' Her eyes darted anxiously about the room, watching for some request for a new bottle, some customer needing help to climb the ladder. She was not seriously considering leaving. The day had been kind enough, in bringing her son back alive. She was not seriously hoping for more.

'What do you mean, "nothing"? Where are today's takings?' Haoyou prised open her hand, felt in her apron pocket: both were stuffed with money.

'That's not mine! They search me every day, to see I'm keeping nothing back! I have to obey them!' Qing'an was panicking. She made one last feeble attempt to recover control of the situation. 'Gou Haoyou, you are a bad, disobedient boy! I forbid you to take that!'

But Haoyou had stopped considering debts of obedience. What had obedience got to do with this gloomy, seedy, underground world? His only duty was to his mother and his sister. 'I know somewhere we can go. No one will think to look for us there. We'll travel down

194

the coast—somewhere no one knows us—and I'll make kites again and find you a house . . . Fetch Wawa!'

His mother, who, by contrast, had learned to do exactly as she was told, obeyed without question. She climbed the ladder and reappeared five minutes later with Wawa asleep in her arms. She had no luggage but one old red shirt which had once belonged to her dead husband. Anything else of value, Uncle Bo had gambled away.

Meanwhile, Haoyou had pulled furniture back from the cellar door and was prising it open with a marlin spike taken from one of the stupefied customers, a sailor. They crept up the cellar steps, looked right and left, and were away down the street long before the doorkeepers came in search of the boy who had pushed past them earlier.

'Where are we going?' howled Qing'an, terrified, struggling under the weight of Wawa. (Haoyou could hardly believe how tall his sister had grown; how silent and withdrawn.) He led them down to the harbour steps and out across the decks of houseboats, merchant boats, fishing junks. Qing'an was white-eyed with terror: the sunlight, the noise, the glittering fissures of water over which he made her step.

Letting go the painter of a little dinghy, Haoyou managed to make it drift abeam of a decaying houseboat moored near the mouth of the harbour. Sun-bleached and mouldy, its hull scraped by big cargo ships and washed about by tides, it had squatted there unoccupied all this while: First Mate Di Chou's houseboat. It was as damp as an otter's holt. Spiders and seabirds, thieves, mildew, and the typhoon had all done their worst. But at least it was empty, and at least it was afloat. Haoyou spent their stolen money on new blankets, a sack of rice, some beans, and cooking fuel, then went to earth with his mother and sister: in hiding, with a price on his head put there by the owners of the drinking den.

And yet he could not bring himself to leave Dagu. Just as the ropes tethering the mildewy hulk to its neighbouring boats had become hopelessly tangled, so Haoyou's thoughts had become twined round the idea of Uncle Bo and Auntie Mo. He was sure his uncle would head for home eventually, certain that they would meet again. Traitor, gambler, cheat, liar: there was not a name Haoyou did not call his absent uncle. At night, lying awake in Di Chou's hammock, he nursed and fed his anger. Like a typhoon it circled his brain faster and faster, until it was the whirling, destructive core at the heart of everything he did and thought.

But it was not Uncle Bo who came home first to Dagu from foreign parts.

It was Di Chou.

21

Fingers

O ne day, Haoyou made his daily check of the house, and returned to the dockside just in time to see his arch enemy descending the jetty steps to a coracle. So. While better men had drowned, Di Chou had survived the typhoon; perhaps the sea had no stomach for him, either. Now he was heading out towards his houseboat, to resume his water-rat's existence scavenging about the waterfront for what work the ships would bring his way. Impossible to reach the houseboat ahead of Chou. Impossible to stop him finding Qing'an and Wawa aboard such a small craft.

'Hoi! Di Chou, you old ox! I thought you were dead!' He shouted it at the top of his voice. Stevedores stopped in their tracks to look at Haoyou.

It had the necessary effect. Di Chou turned and saw the boy he blamed for all his recent sufferings: the one who had shanghaied him aboard a ship on the eve of his marriage. The surprise gave Haoyou a momentary advantage; he could have turned tail and run. But what good would that do his mother? Instead he held his ground, vaguely wondering if the first mate would dare to kill him here, in so public a place.

He did not have long to wait for his answer. Drawing his knife, Di Chou came at him as if Haoyou were a door to be broken down. They dodged this way and that around bollards and crates: a deadly game of peek-a-boo. 'Where's that other one that helped you? The girl. The medium.'

'Don't know. Gone. Married. Long gone,' Haoyou panted.

The knife slashed and jabbed. 'And that mother of yours?'

'Wouldn't you like to know.'

'That only leaves you, then!'

There was nothing for it but to jump backwards off the edge of the dock, to drop feet-first into the filthy sink of the harbour. He fell in among the offal from the gutting tables, the litter from the houseboats, among the tangled mooring ropes and floating tar. Children laughed to see the splash he made, and watched with curiosity as he floundered and gasped. His shoes came off and sank into the darkness beneath him.

Di Chou bent his head down towards the water so that his heavy jowls swelled out his cheeks. 'I can wait! I can wait!' he called down, leering and jeering. 'What's it to be? Stay there and drown or get out and be cut into fishbait?'

Where was the man with the white whip now, to rescue him, or the riders with the blue shirts? Where was Mipeng to put courage in him? Where was his father who had kept the world safe for a little boy? What could be done? What could any of them do? Even the oil-slippery Uncle Bo could not have extricated himself from a predicament like this. Or could he?

'I'll wager you!'

'You what?'

'You like a bet, don't you? A gamble? Well, then, I'll play you! I win and you let me live. I lose and you get . . . all the money I earned flying kites. You must've heard! I made a good living. Flew for Kublai Khan himself! I'm Phoenix! I'm Sun Swallow!' Something brushed against him under the water: a knot of eels, maybe, or a dead dog. He did not think he could tread water much longer. 'It's

198

hidden. You kill me, and you don't get a penny of it. But if you play me . . . ' The lie grew inside him, a cold lump under his quaking diaphragm. 'I'm the only one left now! The rest are all dead! I'm head of the Gou family now! I have property! What have you got to lose? They can behead you for murder, but they can't touch you for winning a bet!' It came out sounding whining and cowardly, but that was all to the good. Di Chou could not resist inflicting fear. 'You wiped me out before, didn't you? What have you got to lose? That's your line of work, isn't it? Getting something for nothing?'

The wash of a passing boat slopped in at his mouth. It tasted of offal.

So it was that Haoyou found himself at the gaming house behind the fishmarket, sitting at a gaming table, making a pool of water around his bare feet, as he shivered in his wet rags. Di Chou's oversized feet, still overlapping the same skimpy sandals, rested on top of Haoyou's. There was a continuous clicking of polished stone dice mingled with the gentle tinkling of money changing hands.

Quite a crowd had followed them up from the harbour, witnesses to the strange bet, the odd one-way gamble. They had never seen anyone stake their life on a bet before.

'Thing is . . . ' said Di Chou, relishing the dismay he had caused the old men who normally sat at the tables, 'thing is, I don't play this old woman's game.' He lifted the corner of the table, and the polished stones slid off into the grass, like rabbit droppings. 'This isn't my game.'

'Why? Can't you count as high as six?'

Di Chou plucked at his wet lower lip. His big knife lay unsheathed on the table. He fingered it like cutlery. Beside it, he laid down his necklace of lucky charms: a declaration that he meant to win. A mummified stoat looked up at Haoyou from among the amulets and mascots, one eye missing. A shrivelled vole shed one claw. 'Fingers! Best of eleven,' said Di Chou. 'You guess first.'

A frisson of excitement went through the crowd at the prospect of such a crucial bet riding on a school-yard game, quickly played, soon over. A blanket was fetched from somewhere and laid over the table. Beneath it, the players' right hands moved like subterranean creatures. 'Now help me, Papa,' said Haoyou inwardly to his father's spirit.

When the cloth was whipped away, Chou's hand lay flat on the table, all five fingers extended. Haoyou's showed only three.

'I win,' said Di Chou, baring his snaggled teeth, and his hand covered Haoyou's, and squeezed until it seemed all the knuckles would crumble.

Word quickly spread that an unusual wager was underway at the gambling house, and the crowd around the table grew bigger and more outspoken.

'What you gonna win off a beggar like that, Chou? Fleas?'

'What you bidding, Chou? Ringworm and a dose of lice?'

It was almost uncanny, the bad luck that fell to Haoyou in that fuggy room in the gambling house. He lost six out of seven rounds, and the growing crowd groaned to see the stubby, tattooed, calloused fingers do combat with the slight, white trembling fingers of the dripping kite-boy.

'Where's this money, then, wind-tester?' demanded Di Chou, triumphant.

'Under the floor in my uncle's house,' mumbled Haoyou. There was a general movement towards the door.

'Wait! Wait! I'll play you again! Double or quits! For the house! For the whole house! If I win, I keep my money!'

Now at last Haoyou knew the hot excitement his great-uncle had found at all those gaming tables, all those dice games, all those wagers about the kite. He could feel it, too—a rim of fire under his ribcage.

Someone came pushing through the crowd, calling him by name, by his real name. 'Haoyou, what are you doing? You can't do this! You don't have to give him anything! What are you doing in a place like this?' It was Mipeng.

Haoyou jumped up. 'Ah! Cousin! Come here! You're just the person!' He grabbed hold of her wrists and squeezed so tightly that she yelped. 'You be my hands!' and he tried to post her hands underneath the blanket.

Some of the crowd (who knew Mipeng as a medium) were incensed. Use a soothsayer to win a game of fingers? It was cheating, surely? But Di Chou only licked his lip with malice. Now he could settle his score with the other brat who had carried him aboard the *Namchi*. 'You told me this one was long gone. But here she is.'

Not for a moment did Haoyou release his grip on Mipeng's wrists. He knew he was twisting her skin painfully; he willed her to understand why.

When Mipeng also lost, the crowd yelped with laughter. Fancy! A medium who could not predict how many fingers her opponent would show! She could not be much of a medium!

'Maybe the spirits won't tell her,' said someone. 'Maybe they favour Chou.' And private bets began to pass between the spectators, some betting on Chou (because the spirits seemed to favour him) some on Haoyou, thinking that luck so bad must surely be about to change.

But it did not change. Even with Mipeng's hands choosing the numbers and Di Chou guessing them, the games still went to him: five games to three, with three draws.

'I've got myself a house!' exclaimed Di Chou, starting to play to the gallery, starting to wear his good luck rakishly, like a new cap. 'Puts me in mind of that other house of yours, kite-maker,' he jeered. 'You remember? All those pretty kites. Didn't they make a cosy blaze?'

'Another game!' cried Haoyou, lifting his head off the table. 'Double or quits!'

The first mate stood up. 'You don't have anything else I want.'

'Oh yes, I do!'

They looked at one another: two enemies in thrall to their hatred, two gamblers addicted to their sport. Mipeng gave a shrill cry and pulled free. 'No, Haoyou! You can't!' He did not even turn to look at her.

'One more game. If I lose, you can marry my mother, Qing'an.'

The room drew in a single breath. Mipeng kicked out at her cousin, shrieking, *'Stop it! Don't! Didn't that fool Bo teach you anything?'*

'Yes. He taught me how to gamble. What about it, Di Chou? I'm head of the Gou household now. I can say yeah or nay to a wedding. My mother's yours, if you win her . . . except you won't. My luck's changing. I feel it. I'll win it all back—the house, the money, everything. What about it?'

Di Chou snorted and blew his nose between his fingers. He tried to read the lie beyond Haoyou's face. 'The woman might be dead for all I know. I been gone months . . .'

'She isn't dead. I swear it. I was with her this morning. What do you say, Di Chou? Give me a chance. I've lost everything. Give me a chance to win it back! You want

202

her, don't you? You killed my father to get hold of her. So she must be worth the risk?'

The crowd hit fever-pitch at the mention of murder. Here was an afternoon to talk about for years to come! They had seen hardened gamblers ruin themselves before, bidding their last coin, their family heirlooms, the jackets off their backs. But they had never seen a boy bid his own *mother*. They began to hiss, restless and noisy as the sea breaking among pebbles. Some were hissing Haoyou for the wrong he was doing his mother, some were hissing Di Chou, remembering Gou Pei's death, believing what the boy said about murder.

On and off the cloth flapped, uncovering the two hands as rigid in their gestures as the hands of dead sailors washed up on a beach.

Three plays four!

One plays five!

Five plays three!

Haoyou no longer tried to concentrate—to guess Di Chou's pattern of play. He simply closed his eyes and shaped his hand, keeping his eyes shut, unable to tell, from the gasps of the crowd, who had won and who had lost. Reaching across, he inadvertently touched the string of animal parts, and a dead cat's head rolled into the palm of his hand: Death in his grasp. Then he felt Di Chou's hand cover his own, clammy with sweat, and crush it, so that the cat's skull was crushed within his palm.

'He wins!' roared the crowd, and Haoyou dropped his head on to his arms, hiding his face.

'*Bring her,*' said Di Chou.

There was a clatter of feet as the crowd parted to let Di Chou pass: the man of property, the man of means, the happy bridegroom.

22

Family

'Happy now?' said Mipeng's voice, trembling with scorn. 'I thought you were dead, Gou Haoyou. I thought you were still with Kublai Khan or dead in the ground. After today, I think I'd rather you were.'

Haoyou lifted his head off his arms. His eyes darted around the suddenly empty room. Then he jumped to his feet and grasped Mipeng firmly by the elbows. 'Now! Quick! Go to the warehouse and tell them: if they want to get back some stolen goods, to go to Bo's house. No, no . . . on second thoughts, I'll go there. You go to the house—the drinking den, you know? I daren't. Tell them, if they want the money Qing'an took, they can *get it back off her betrothed.*'

Mipeng, white-faced, swayed a little as she tried to deduce why Haoyou was so cheerful.

Then she brightened like morning. 'You wanted to lose!' she murmured. 'You needed to lose!' Her hand moved to the crown of her stomach. 'I don't like to run these days,' she said.

But she did.

The supervisors at the warehouse arrived at Bo's neglected house to find the floorboards up and First Mate Di Chou squatting among his winnings: stolen hanks of raw silk, cakes of incense, tea and buttons, a roll of creamy blank paper, cooking oil, cinnamon sticks, brass spoons, fireworks, cowhide belts, hairpins, animal horn, fish line, and rice wine. They recognized it well enough: it had been pilfered from them over the space of the past three years. 'Arrest the thief,' they said.

When they would not listen to his explanation, Chou lashed out with his fists and made a run for it. But as he plunged out of the window, he came face-to-face with the club-wielding debt-collectors from the drinking den. 'Are you the betrothed of Gou Qing'an?' they wanted to know.

'Yes, yes!' he agreed, then stared uncomprehendingly at their open palms as they demanded back their stolen money, with menaces.

If witnesses could have been found to testify to Di Chou's innocence, he might have fared better. But witnesses were a breed unknown to the Dagu waterfront. No one spoke up for Di Chou. No one stepped in to save him from the fists and clubs of the debt-collectors.

All unwitting, Gou Bo returned to his plundered house the following week, and was aghast to find it broken open, his cache of pilfered goodies gone. He and Auntie Mo sat side by side, like a bag of washing beside a bag of pegs. They did not comment on the hole in the floor. Mo had always known about it, and Bo had always known she knew, but neither knew now how to comment on the loss of their ill-gotten gains.

Mo's face had grown so long and anxious over the past few months that it seemed to be flowing downwards into her weary old body like an hourglass emptying of sand. 'Will they take you back at the warehouse, do you think?' she asked.

'It's not right for a man of my years to be toting bales and boxes,' said Bo. He meant he was too old and untrustworthy to be given back his job.

'We still have the ox-cart,' said Mo. She meant that he could perhaps work as a carrier, a delivery man.

'Yes, yes. We have the ox-cart.' He meant that he would sell it the next day and use the proceeds to gamble at the gaming tables. No one in Dagu knew what had happened during his weeks away. No one knew. No one knew. And Bo reasoned that if no one knew, it was almost as if nothing had happened at all. Almost as if he had never been away.

They bedded down on the broken slats of the floor and, when he stirred, Bo imagined he must still be out-of-doors, under the stars. For there was a pale disc above him, like a full moon. Then it resolved itself into a face.

'You! You're dead! Get away! Leave me alone!' He could not make his strangled voice loud enough to wake his wife who only groaned in her sleep.

Another ghost joined the first—a moon part eclipsed by dark crescents of hair.

'You're dead! You're both dead! What do you want with me? Leave me alone!'

Mo finally woke, thinking the barbarians had come, to murder her in her sleep. Instead, she found her husband's face buried in her stomach, his tears hot through her wrap. The moon was strong through the unplanked window, and beside her squatted Haoyou and Mipeng. Her hand rose to her wisps of grey, louse-flecked hair. 'Praise be to the gods and all our ancestors! The Khan let you go!' she whispered. Then she hugged Mipeng to her breast, and wept, for the first time, at the awfulness of everything that had happened.

'It's time to leave Dagu, Auntie,' said Haoyou.

Bo emerged, slow to shake off the notion of ghosts, blustering his way out of his mistake like a man pushing through cobwebs. 'Leave? Leave? We're going nowhere! You, boy! Do you have the kite, still?'

'No, Great-Uncle. It broke. It was smashed to pieces. My eye, too. I'm blind in one eye.'

Bo reflected for only a moment. 'No matter. We can soon build another. Now, wait outside until I summon you. You, girl! I have to ask: is this any time of night to be out-of-doors? You know my wife and I do not receive guests in the middle of the night. Nothing honest was ever done after dark.' He swept his dirty, uncut hair flat against his skull, his plump lids drooping, hoping to conceal the delight even now swelling in his throat. 'I must ponder the family's future!' he intoned, gathering his old pomposity around him like unpacked baggage. Rolling his bottom on hard planks, where there had once been a cushion to sit on, he drew in his legs and crossed them. The whole man seemed to swell like a great toad restored to its pond after drought. 'This once, Mipeng, I am willing to overlook your unseemly behaviour. Tomorrow we must let it be known you are back in Dagu: available for seances and fortune-telling. I would wrong our ancestors if I were to waste your skills as a medium.'

'Oh, but Bo,' said Auntie Mo tentatively, 'would she not be of more use to you here? At home? Cooking and cleaning?' Bo ignored her.

'I find that, just at present, I do not have the capital I need to re-equip the boy. It is up to you to earn enough to buy wood and silk as quickly as possible. So, in the morning . . . '

'No, Uncle,' said Mipeng. She did not raise her voice, but she was quietly insistent. 'I have no gift as a medium. Thanks to Haoyou, I proved it, up at the gambling house last week. "Gou Mipeng is no medium." Everyone is saying so. Besides . . . my husband would not approve of me earning money that way.'

Bo's eyes bulged so far out of his head that he looked in danger of bursting. *'Your what?'*

'We wished your blessing,' said Mipeng, bowing

her head contritely. 'But you were not there for us to ask it.'

Bo rolled forward on to his hands and knees to peer more closely into her face. His jowls quivered. 'You *married*? And whom, pray, do you think you have married?'

'The man you call Miao Jié, Uncle,' replied Mipeng in her softest, lowest voice. 'The Kublai Khan spared his life. As you see. We were not galloped to death in the carpet. He has gone to fetch Qing'an and Wawa out of hiding, and take them on board . . . '

Bo rolled upright again, and interrupted her with a sharp clap which summoned her closer. 'All's well, then. All's well.' The corners of his mouth rose in a Buddha's beatific smile. His wife gave a gasping laugh of relief, at her husband's calm reaction. Mipeng, startled, crawled closer to receive the blessing of her family patriarch which every bride craves . . .

. . . And Bo's hands closed round her throat.

'There is no marriage without permission,' he stated categorically. Mipeng could say nothing. His thumbs were on her windpipe. 'You have brought shame on the family. Brought shame on the respectable name of Gou. I am within my rights—indeed, it is my *duty*, as head of the family, to strangle you here and now as a wayward—'

'*Husband!*' Mo beat on her husband's back with the first thing that came to hand: the fly whisk. His patriarchal smile did not so much as falter. Stray strands of Mipeng's hair quivered in the moonlight.

'It is not as if I did not give you due warning,' he said, his voice rising and falling in a matter-of-fact sing-song banter. 'I have had to speak to you often in the past. But now the time for words is past.'

Mo screamed for Haoyou, and Haoyou ran back in from

the yard. He saw a shape in the moonlight he could not make sense of at first: upraised elbows, upraised hands, Mo beating with the fly whisk.

'Great-Uncle, no!'

Noises came from Mipeng's throat which made the little house sound haunted by chickens long since stolen.

'Uncle, no! She's with child! She's expecting a baby! A royal baby!'

Bo was not listening. 'You may, perhaps, have dirtied your soul, Gou Mipeng, but you have not, I assure you, married anybody at all . . . '

Mo wheezed frantically—little panting breaths—taken on Mipeng's behalf. Bo shook his niece so hard that her head rocked forward and cracked him in the mouth, drawing blood.

Haoyou grappled to prise the fingers away from the long white neck, but he might as well have tried to unbend iron nails. So instead, he screamed in at Bo's ear: 'All right! I'll fly for you! I'll build a kite! I will! I bet I can win you a thousand cash a day. I can. I bet you! Only I need Mipeng. I need my medium!'

At that, Bo finally relinquished his hold. Mipeng fell limply across the space where the family shrine should have stood. Bo's rubbery lids closed serenely over his protruding eyes. 'As long as it is clearly understood,' he intoned. 'The first duty of young people is to obey their elders. Without this, Society topples.'

'Yes, yes, husband!' squeaked Mo eagerly. 'They understand all that!'

Mipeng, still unable to speak, rose to her knees, folding both hands around her stomach, as if to shield her unborn child's ears from the news: his duty would always be, first and foremost, to obey his Great-Uncle Bo.

'You may sleep now. In the next room,' said Bo with a generosity which glossed over the lack of beds anywhere in the house. Haoyou and Mipeng left the room, softly, without a word, without demur, the bruised picture of perfect Obedience.

Bo dreamed one more 'dream' before morning. This time the ghost which leaned over him was white not only in face but from head to foot: all pale planes and dark indentations, like the moon itself. Bo whimpered and pulled the bedding over his head.

'Be lucky, Gou Bo. Be lucky.' The Miao's ice-cold fingers pulled down the bedding and pressed two large coins into the sockets of his tightly closed eyes . . .

Consequently, the following morning, Bo woke shaking like a man with malaria. With one hand clenched around the coins, he could not properly hold the cup of tea which he found beside him, but slopped its contents over his sleeping roll.

'Is that unlucky, would you say?' he called, trying to pick the individual tea leaves up with shaking finger tips. But his wife did not answer. At least, no answer came from the next room.

He could not make his prayers before the family shrine, because it was no longer there. That worried him a little. Supposing his ancestors withdrew their help, because he had not propitiated them? So he poured out the remains of the morning tea on to the patch of floor where the shrine had stood before it was stolen, hoping that might count for something. Then he dressed with great care, buttoning alternate buttons from the bottom upwards (because he had always found that brought him luck). He wound himself in his belt, making the turns just so, the knot to the exactly lucky formula he always used when he was going gambling. Then he jingled the two coins in his palm. The noise soothed him. The ghost had, after all, guaranteed him a win. 'Tea! More tea, wife!' he called. But no answer came from beyond the wall. 'Wife Mo? Niece Mipeng? Haoyou?' No answer.

Two hours later, Bo blundered out through the door of the gambling house, his two coins gone, and tottered down to the sea-front. 'Still have the ox-cart,' he said under his breath, and at once began to estimate what he could raise by selling the creaking, rickety vehicle and the wormy, exhausted beast between its shafts. Soon, he could almost feel the proceeds jingling in his pocket, the dice slippery between his fingers. He would show them: the traitors, the absconders, the disobedient scum who had dared to call themselves relations of his. They would not see one cash of his Big Win when it came. Why, he could almost smell his change of luck blowing in on the morning wind, all mixed up with the stench of rotting fish heads and offal.

Out on the bay, beyond the harbour bar, beyond the line where the ocean's colour turned a deeper blue, a great red-sailed junk heeled into the rising wind. It towed behind it a string of little butty boats, so that its silhouette was that of a great dragon: giant head preceding a tapering, articulated tail. The butties were laden with bird cages and crates, hoops and balls and banners. In the wake of this splendid convoy, white gulls jostled, raucous as a circus crowd vying for the best view.

The remaining members of the Jade Circus cooked rice over little metal braziers or clambered in the rigging, or sat about on deck, in the shade of the great sail. Along the rail, a series of little paper kites dried in the balmy wind—

the first of the kites Haoyou would make and sell to the crowds who came to performances. A skilled craft; an honest living.

No Mongol horsemen had been willing to venture far out over the watery blue steppe, believing that their ancestors were landlubbers and hovered only over the dry places. Given the choice, coastal waters were their limit. But those aboard the circus-master's ship: Miao Jié, Mipeng, the dancers and roustabouts, Qing'an and Wawa, the acrobats and jugglers, Haoyou, Auntie Mo, and the magicians were not so confined. Duty done, each according to his conscience, they were free now to go wherever the sea-lanes took them.

Haoyou was well acquainted with the sky. He knew it better than the Mongols. Up there were winds so strong that they must long since have stirred everybody's ancestors—Chinese, Tibetan, Tartar, good, bad, indifferent, and loving—into a single, jumbled, tumbling pageant vaster than Cathay, vaster than the Khanate of Kublai, as edgeless as the sky itself.

A gentle breeze fluttered the paper between his fingers, as if reminding Haoyou of the job in hand. He turned his thoughts back to making kites.

Geraldine McCaughrean is one of the most highly-acclaimed living children's writers. She has won the Carnegie Medal, the Whitbread Children's Book Award (three times), the Guardian Children's Fiction Award, and the Blue Peter Book of the Year Award, and is known and admired for the variety and originality of her books, as well as her stunning storytelling skills.

Among her other books for OUP are *The White Darkness*, *Stop the Train*, and *Not the End of the World*. In 2005 she was chosen by the Trustees of Great Ormond Street Hospital for Children to write the official sequel to *Peter Pan*. The result was *Peter Pan in Scarlet* which was published worldwide to huge critical acclaim in 2006 and became an instant classic.

Neverland is calling again...

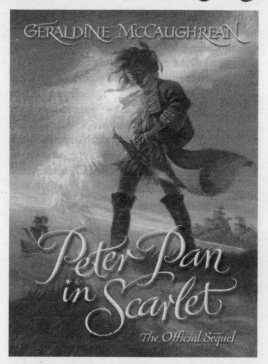

The first ever official sequel to J.M. Barrie's *Peter Pan*

Something is wrong in Neverland. Dreams are leaking out—
strangely real dreams, of pirates and mermaids, of warpaint and
crocodiles. For Wendy and the Lost Boys it is a clear signal—
Peter Pan needs their help, and so it is time to do the
unthinkable and fly to Neverland again.

But back in Neverland, everything has changed—
and the dangers they find there are far
beyond their dreams . . .

Great
Ormond
Street
Hospital
Charity

OXFORD